'I can't understand my mother allowing this situation to happen.' Lucy tossed her head yet again. 'I wish I'd been here.'

'And what would you have done?' Conan sneered. 'Talked her out of marrying my father? Can't you see how much in love they are? Would you deny her that happiness because something unavoidable happened?'

Lucy nearly hit the roof. '*Unavoidable?* Good lord, how can you say that? It was your fault my father died.'

His lips compressed. 'Is that what you think?'

'What else is there to think?' she demanded.

'I did what I had to do.'

'And you didn't care who you hurt in the process? Don't you think you should have made it your business to find out all the facts before you—pressured my father into his grave?'

'I don't think I want to continue this conversation,' he said coldly. 'It's pointless, and it's certainly not the place or the time.'

'There never will be a place or a time,' she snapped, 'because I never want to see you again. I hate your guts, Conan Templeton, and I always will.'

# PRISONER
# OF THE MIND

BY

MARGARET MAYO

**MILLS & BOON LIMITED**
ETON HOUSE    18-24 PARADISE ROAD
RICHMOND    SURREY    TW9 1SR

*First published in Great Britain 1988
by Mills & Boon Limited*

© Margaret Mayo 1988

*Australian copyright 1988
Philippine copyright 1988
This edition 1988*

ISBN 0 263 76137 1

*Set in Times Roman 10 on 12 pt.
01-8811-53097*

Made and printed in Great Britain

# CHAPTER ONE

'OH, MOM, you look marvellous.' Lucy dropped her cases and wrapped her arms around her mother. 'When you wrote and told me about Alan I never dreamt I'd be hearing wedding bells so quickly. I'm dying to meet him. He must be pretty special. You always swore you'd never get married again.'

'And I meant it,' smiled Mrs Anderson. 'I still wonder how it happened, but I'm deliriously happy all the same.' Her eyes shone and she looked younger than she had in years. The delphinium-blue of her dress suited her, and her dark hair with its peppering of grey was freshly cut and blow-dried ready for the big event tomorrow. 'Don't let's stand here on the step. Alan's waiting inside. He's longing to meet you, too.'

It was good to be back, decided Lucy, as she followed her mother into their neat little detached house. Much as she had enjoyed her secretarial course, she missed her home comforts.

Everything looked exactly the same: the red hall carpet, the gleaming mirror and the wooden coat stand. The white walls, always white, right through the house. Her father had said it made decorating easier.

They went into the living-room and there was Alan Templeton, the man who had given her mother a new lease of life. He was tall, with steel-grey hair, kind eyes and a warm smile.

He did not wait for her mother to introduce them. He held out both hands and she readily put hers into them.

'Lucy,' he said, his eyes searching her face. 'You're exactly as I imagined.'

His grasp was warm and firm and Lucy liked him on sight. 'I hope that's a compliment?'

'It certainly is,' he said. 'You look how your mother must have done twenty-five years ago. The same beautiful green eyes, the same high cheekbones, the same thick black hair.' Except that Lucy's was to her shoulders, whereas her mother's was quite short these days. 'You could be sisters, do you know that? I bet you take the same size in clothes?'

Valerie Anderson looked pleased at the compliment, and Lucy decided that Alan Templeton was better-looking than she had imagined also. He was broad-shouldered, in his fifties, yet with no trace of a middle-aged paunch, and he looked as though he would take good care of her parent.

'Well?' said her mother, smiling happily. 'Do you approve?'

Lucy nodded. 'He seems nice.'

'He's more than nice.' Valerie Anderson slid up to the new love in her life and Alan put his arm possessively about her shoulders. Valerie kissed his cheek. 'He's the best thing that could have happened to me.'

And she looked so young and happy and so much in love that Lucy could not agree more. 'I'm pleased for you, Mom. I really am. My congratulations to you both. Is everything ready for tomorrow?'

'You bet,' said her mother.

'I'm so sorry I couldn't be here to help.'

'Heavens, don't worry,' smiled Valerie.

'I wish Conan were here too,' said Alan, a slight shadow crossing his face.

'So you and he could have a stag night?' teased Valerie.

He grimaced. 'At my time of life? No, thanks. But we could have all had a nice quiet family evening getting to know one another.'

Lucy's green eyes twinkled mischievously. 'Are you saying you don't know my mother very well?'

Alan grinned, appreciating her humour. 'I was thinking about you and my son. After all, you will be seeing quite a lot of him.'

A frown creased Lucy's brow and Valerie said quickly, 'I have a surprise for you, darling. I've got you a job as Conan's secretary. You start on Monday. Isn't that wonderful?'

'I do?' Lucy's lovely green eyes widened. It was the first she had heard of it. But it was good news, too.

'You *are* pleased?' asked her mother anxiously. 'I didn't have time to consult you. It all happened so quickly, Conan's secretary leaving, and him desperate to fill her place.'

'Pleased? It's fantastic news. Thanks, Mom, you too, Alan. I never imagined I'd start work so quickly. When will I meet him?'

'Tomorrow,' answered Alan. 'He'll be here early.'

But he wasn't. He phoned to say he was delayed and would go straight to the church. Lucy didn't think much of that. Surely he could have made an effort? It was not every day one's father got married. She wondered exactly what type of man it was she was going to work for.

When he did finally arrive, sliding into the pew behind his father, Lucy looked frowningly across. Alan was tall, but his son was even taller, with a powerful physique and a face that was more interesting than it was handsome. It was rugged and craggy, and deeply tanned, as though he had just come back from holiday.

He whispered a few words over his father's shoulder, and then the wedding march began and all conversation ceased.

Her mother looked beautiful in an ivory silk two-piece, and her eyes were full of love as she took her place at Alan's side. Alan wore a pale grey suit and they made a handsome couple. Lucy felt a lump in her throat as they exchanged their vows. Her mother deserved this. She had been devastated when her husband had died, and Lucy had never thought to see her happy again.

She glanced at Conan Templeton and saw that he was watching them also. But not so intently that he did not feel her gaze on him. He turned his head slowly and their eyes met, and Lucy had the vaguest feeling that she had seen him somewhere before.

It puzzled her, and she searched the recesses of her mind, but came up with nothing. For some reason, though, he disturbed her, and she felt sure the memories were not happy ones.

He was a very attractive man. His eyes were as dark as his hair, half hooded at this moment, as if he too were wondering about her. And why shouldn't he? She was going to work for him. He must be equally interested.

Lucy found it difficult to concentrate on the service. She knew this man, but how? Where had they met? When? Under what circumstances? She felt oddly uneasy and not at all sure that she now wanted to work for him. Her questions were still unanswered when Alan introduced them at the reception.

'Conan, this is Lucy, whom you've heard so much about. Lucy, my son.'

Lucy took the younger man's hand and felt the warmth and strength of his grasp, and she looked into the depths of his black eyes. They were regarding her steadily, disconcertingly, and once again she wished she could re-member what was bugging her about him.

His full mouth widened into a smile, revealing even, white teeth, and softening the somewhat austere lines of his face. 'How like your mother you are.'

He had a deep, gravelly, sensual voice that throbbed from somewhere deep in his stomach and must have melted many a girl's bones. But still Lucy could not dispel her misgivings. 'So I've been told,' she said, and there was no answering smile on her lips.

A faint frown grooved his tanned brow, but his friendly tone gave nothing away. 'What do you think of these parents of ours getting married? I'd begun to think my father would never find anyone else.'

Alan gave his son a playful cuff about the ears before moving on, and there was no disputing the excellent camaraderie between the two of them.

'I'm very pleased,' said Lucy politely. 'It's good to see my mother happy again.' She paused and then said, 'I believe I have to thank you for giving me a job. You're very kind.' She said the words but did not mean them. Kindness was not part of this man's character, she felt sure. 'But you didn't have to. Just because Mom put in a good word, there was no need for——'

'You don't want the job?' he cut in with an abrupt frown. 'Fair enough. There are plenty of girls who do.'

His sharp tone incensed Lucy and, perversely, she decided that she did want the job, after all. She would be a fool to turn it down in these days of high unem-ployment. 'It's not that,' she protested. 'Of course I want it. It's just that—I don't like having plans made for me. I'm twenty-three, perfectly capable of conducting my own life. Would you excuse me, please; I've just spotted a friend who I haven't seen in ages. I must have a word with her.'

She walked away, conscious of her mother's frown of annoyance that she was leaving Conan's side so soon, but even more conscious of the impact this man had made on her. If it weren't for this strange feeling that there was something wrong, she would have been quite attracted to him. He was easily the most physical man she had ever met.

And then, suddenly, half an hour later, it came to her. She was discreetly watching him and there was something about the exact angle of his head that struck a chord in her mind.

She had never met Conan Templeton, no, but she had seen his picture in the local *Advertiser*. His company's name had been on her father's tongue often enough. How could she have forgotten him? She knew enough about him to make her throat tighten in anger, her fingers curl into fists, and her senses burn with outrage.

This was the man who had taken her father to court. This was the man who had caused him to have a heart attack. *Conan Templeton had killed her father!* Not by his own hands, but by his accusations, his slander, his power in the business world. Did her mother know? God, it didn't bear thinking about.

But she couldn't ask her mother at this moment. She couldn't spoil her day. She wished with all her heart, though, that Valerie and Alan had never met. What a cruel quirk of fate. There was no way she could work for Conan Templeton now. She never wanted to speak to him again.

He looked suddenly across and Lucy could not hide her hatred. It flashed from her eyes like a gamma ray. If any man should be dead, it was he. She had loved her

father dearly, and had grieved for a long time following
his death two years ago.

Conan Templeton's eyes narrowed, but when he
headed in her direction Lucy deliberately moved away.
And she somehow managed to avoid him until her
mother and Alan left for their luxury honeymoon cruise,
and the guests departed, and all that remained was for
them to go home. Then she could avoid him no longer.
Nor did she want to. She had plenty to say to Conan
Templeton.

'I've realised who you are,' she spat, her eyes blazing
as she turned to him. 'Does my mother know?'

His lips quirked with amusement. 'Of course. Can I
give you a lift home?'

'No, thanks,' she said tightly. 'My mother's a fool if
she's forgiven you. I certainly am not so soft-hearted.'

'So I see. It was quite a shock, wasn't it, when you
recognised me?'

'You can say that again.' Lucy tossed her head so
fiercely that her green pillbox hat flew off and her thick,
shiny dark hair swung about her face.

Conan bent down and picked up her hat, and was
about to replace it solemnly when she snatched it from
him, crushing it between her hands, wishing it were his
skull.

'You're ruining it,' he pointed out calmly.

'As if I care,' she spat back. 'I shan't ever wear it
again, or this suit.' She looked down at the pale green
silk skirt and jacket, with its toning blouse. It had been
horrendously expensive, but she had thought it worth
it. 'Because if I do,' she went on, 'it will remind me of
you. And you're the last person I want to think about.'

'That's a pity,' he said, and she thought he meant the bit about her not wanting to think about him, but he continued smoothly, 'It looks good on you.'

He insolently appraised the long, slender length of her legs, clad in pale green stockings too, her shoes a darker shade. She had bought the whole outfit in London and had felt like a million dollars. He halted briefly on the thrust of her breasts, and then met her eyes once again. She looked at him stonily, her lips clamped tightly together, her whole body screaming her aggression.

'I can't understand my mother allowing this situation to happen.' She tossed her head yet again. 'I wish I'd been here.'

'And what would you have done?' he sneered. 'Talked her out of marrying my father? Can't you see how much in love they are? Would you deny her that happiness because something unavoidable happened?'

Lucy nearly hit the roof. *'Unavoidable?* Good lord, how can you say that? It was your fault my father died.'

His lips compressed. 'Is that what you think?'

'What else is there to think?' she demanded.

'I did what I had to do.'

'And you didn't care who you hurt in the process? Don't you think you should have made it your business to find out all the facts before you—pressurised my father into his grave?'

'I don't think I want to continue this conversation,' he said coldly. 'It's pointless, and it's certainly not the place or the time.'

'There never will be a place or a time,' she snapped, 'because I never want to see you again. I hate your guts, Conan Templeton, and I always will.'

She turned her back on him and walked away, but he caught her arm and spun her to face him. 'I think you're forgetting that you're my new secretary.'

'Like hell I am! You can keep your job, I don't want it.'

He looked at her insolently. 'I didn't cast you as the type to go back on your word.'

Lucy's hackles rose. 'I'm not.'

'Good.' His smile was triumphant. 'Nine o'clock sharp on Monday, then?'

Lucy glared, her whole body boiling. But what could she do?

'You really should take a leaf out of your mother's book,' he continued smoothly.

'My mother needs her head examining,' retorted Lucy. 'Although perhaps it shouldn't surprise me, her forgiving you. She's the kindest, warmest, most gentle woman you're ever likely to meet. My father was the same.'

He nodded, as though he knew. Yet how could he? Was he humouring her? God, she hated him.

'I think we ought to leave,' he said. 'They're waiting to clear up.'

Without conscious thought Lucy walked by his side out of the restaurant and across to the car park. 'My father took the blame, did you know that?' she questioned heatedly. 'He felt sorry for Martin Goodfellow, would you believe? Sorry for him because he had an invalid wife.' Her lip curled in anger. 'I will never, ever, if I live to be a hundred, understand how he could forgive a man who swindled him out of so much money.'

They reached his car, a black Porsche Carrera with a wide gold band running along either side, and the word Porsche in big gold letters. Lucy would have been impressed if she hadn't been so upset. He unlocked the door and held it open. 'I believe the man was a life-long friend of your father?'

'Some friend, when he's still alive and my father's dead,' she spat.

He took her arm and urged her into the car, and she decided, why not? Her own car was at home and it would save calling a taxi.

'Martin Goodfellow also had a mistress,' she informed him tightly, once he was in beside her and the car's engine purred into life. 'And my father knew nothing about it. I guess he wouldn't have been so generous if he'd known Martin had fled the country with another woman.'

Conan shrugged, as if her disclosure was of no interest. But of course it wouldn't be. He didn't care about people's feelings. All he cared about was money and power and success. Whom he trod on in the process was of no concern to him.

There was a tense silence between them on the short journey. It was a powerful car, comfortable, compact. Too compact. Lucy would have liked more space between them.

Conan was not the type of man you could ignore. He was totally masculine, exuding an animal virility that even in her hostility she could not dismiss. How old was he? Thirty-four, thirty-five? Was he married? Was——

'What are you thinking?'

Conan's voice broke into her thoughts. She turned her head and met the smoky darkness of his eyes. 'I was wondering whether you had a wife,' she admitted coolly.

His brows rose. 'Should I be flattered that you're interested?'

'I'm not,' she crisped. 'It was an idle thought, no more. But if you do have a wife, then I pity her from the bottom of my heart.'

'You think I'm too ruthless to make a good husband?' She nodded.

His lips twisted wryly. 'There is no Mrs Templeton, and there's no one permanent in my life at the moment. Does that satisfy your curiosity?'

Lucy shrugged. 'I wasn't really interested.'

Disbelief flickered in his eyes, and she was relieved when the journey ended. Almost before the car stopped on the drive, Lucy's fingers were on the handle, and she scrambled out. 'Thank you for the lift, Mr Templeton.'

At the front door she searched in her handbag for her key, and then remembered to her dismay that she had forgotten to transfer it from her other bag. What a fool.

Conan appeared suddenly and silently behind her, dangling a key on a ring, a mocking smile on his lips. 'Perhaps I can be of assistance?'

Lucy frowned. 'Where did you get that from?'

'Your mother gave it to me.'

'Why?'

'In case I ever needed it.'

'Why would you need a key to our house?'

'Isn't it obvious, Lucy?' he said with exaggerated patience. 'My father is moving in here, so this will be my family home as well.'

Lucy's heart stopped beating. 'You mean, you're thinking of *living* here?'

He smiled at her obvious consternation. 'How I would love to shock you and say yes. But no, I have my own place.' He turned the key in the lock. 'Shall we go in?'

Lucy had no choice. He was taking over. She stepped inside and he followed and the door closed quietly behind them.

Immediately the house seemed filled with his presence. She walked through into the kitchen, taking off her jacket and hanging it over the back of a chair, trying to ignore him but finding it impossible. She opened the fridge and poured herself a glass of milk, drinking half of it in one go, then eyeing him stonily.

He was leaning nonchalantly against the door-jamb, his tie loosened, his hands thrust into his trouser-pockets. His navy suit was immaculate, his white shirt still as fresh as when he'd arrived at the church.

'Tell me,' she said, 'is Alan part of C.T. Steels?'

His eyes narrowed. 'You think he had a hand in your father's downfall?'

'Nothing would surprise me any longer,' she rasped.

'Actually,' he said, 'he is on the board of directors. But he doesn't play an active part these days.'

As far as Lucy was concerned, if Alan Templeton was connected with the company, no matter how remotely, he was as good as involved.

'Your mother first met him at a meeting of the creditors—when she was helping to sort out your father's affairs.'

*'What?'* exploded Lucy. 'She didn't tell me.'

'And I can see why,' he retorted scathingly. 'You're a very hard girl, Lucy Anderson.'

'If you hadn't taken legal action against my father, he would be alive now,' she accused.

'He owed us money.'

'Martin Goodfellow owed you money, not my father,' she raged, her eyes flashing fire, her whole body stiff with aggression. 'Don't you *care* that my father's firm meant everything to him? It was his life. He built it up from nothing. And even when he could afford to let others do the work for him he still worked alongside his men. He wasn't a figurehead, sitting back and counting his money.'

'Maybe he should have been. Goodfellow didn't do him any favours.'

Lucy finished her milk and slammed the glass back down on the table. 'My father had no brain for that side of the business. He openly admitted that. He trusted Martin and they had plenty of good years together. It's my guess Martin got greedy when he found himself a mistress. He set her up in her own house, do you know that? She wanted for nothing—and all financed by my father's money.'

'If it hadn't been me who took him to court it would have been someone else,' Conan said.

'Rubbish!' snorted Lucy indelicately. 'He bought all his steel from you. What he owed anyone else was peanuts. Couldn't you have eased off? Let him sort things out without taking him to court?'

'I wish I could have done. But that isn't the way the business world operates.'

'Don't I know it,' groaned Lucy. 'But Martin had gone before we knew anything about it, and my father insisted on taking the blame. He was like that. I'd be obliged if you'd leave. I really have no wish to prolong this conversation.'

'Aren't you going to at least offer me a cup of tea?' His lips quirked his amusement at her displeasure. 'Or shall I make it myself? I don't mind.'

'I'll do it,' snapped Lucy. She did not want him making himself at home. 'Perhaps you'd like to go through to the lounge?'

'I'll stay here,' he said, 'and watch you. I can't make up my mind whether you're more beautiful when you're angry or when you're smiling.'

She ignored him, filling the kettle and switching it on, getting the cups ready, all the time fuming over the way he had marched in.

How could her mother have fixed up this job for her? Valerie must have known how she would react once she discovered who Conan really was. Lucy had loved her father dearly. When she was little her mother had been ill for a long time and he had looked after her. He had played with her, loved her, washed her, dressed her; they had done everything together, and consequently they had developed a closeness that had never gone away. Lucy made no secret of the fact that she did not want to hear ever again the name of the firm who had taken him to court. It was anathema to her. And indeed, it had not been mentioned in the whole of the two years since her father's death.

Why, then, had her mother struck up a friendship with Alan Templeton? And, even more to the point, why had she allowed it to develop? How could she love this man who was part and parcel of the company who had ruined their business? None of it made any sense.

Her mother had been heartbroken when Eric died, absolutely devastated. She had gone completely to pieces, so how could she forgive Alan Templeton to the extent of marrying him? Lucy could not understand it.

The kettle boiled and she made the tea. Conan picked up the tray and carried it through into the lounge. He knew the way, confirming that he had been here before. The thought rankled, and Lucy's face was grim as she sat down in front of the low table and picked up the pot.

'Why did you wait until you were twenty-one to begin your secretarial training?'

His question took her by surprise. 'You mean my mother hasn't told you? How surprising. I seem to have been very much under discussion. Actually I left school at sixteen, deciding I'd had enough of education and wanted to go into the big outside world.'

His lips quirked but he said nothing, just watched her with his dark, perceptive eyes.

'My parents were naturally disappointed because they wanted me to go to college. But I thought I knew best. I learned the hard way that jobs weren't easy to come by unless you were qualified. I jumped from dead-end job to dead-end job, and it wasn't until my father died that I realised how much I could have helped my mother if I'd had a good job.'

'So who paid for your secretarial course? It was a private college?'

'I had a legacy from an aunt,' she admitted. 'I wanted to give my mother the money, but she insisted I put it to good use. I was worried about leaving her so soon after Daddy died, and I used to come home every weekend, but eventually she picked up the threads of her life and I only came at the end of each term.'

'And now you're a fully qualified secretary. You've been trained on computers and word processors, as well as all the old skills?'

Lucy nodded.

'I think we should get on well. What are you doing tomorrow?'

The unexpected question startled Lucy. 'Resting,' she said flatly, sliding his tea across the table towards him.

'We could spend the day together. Perhaps go up on the moors and resolve our differences?'

'You're a born optimist, aren't you?' Lucy grated. 'It's enough that I'm committed to working for you. I don't want to see you in my own time as well. I shall never, *ever* forget what you did to my father. So far as I'm concerned you're a *murderer*.' She spat the word angrily. 'Please drink your tea and go.'

Conan's face tightened and his eyes were glacial. 'Perhaps you'll soon learn that the cut and thrust of the business world does not take individuals into account. It was your father's company I took to court, not your father. I liked him. He was a little too soft-hearted to be a businessman, but he was a good man for all that. I was sorry when I heard that he had died.'

'I bet you were,' sneered Lucy. 'I bet you didn't lose one wink of sleep over it. I bet you didn't even connect his death with what you had done to him.'

He shook his head. 'This conversation is getting us nowhere, not in the mood you're in. I think you're right, I should go. Perhaps on Monday you'll be in a more receptive mood?'

'I don't think so.' Her green eyes flashed her dislike.

'You're wrong, you know,' he said, standing up. 'It's fatal to let hatred fester. Before you know it you'll find it's affecting everything you do.'

'That will be my bad luck,' Lucy hissed, springing savagely to her feet. She crossed to the door and yanked it open, marched down the hall and flung that door open too. Then she stood back for him to leave.

When he was level with her he stopped and smiled. His eyes crinkled at the corners and his mouth softened. He appeared not at all concerned by her outburst. 'It's a pity we've got off on the wrong foot,' he said softly.

'Your opinion, not mine,' she snapped.

He leaned towards her, and Lucy was taken completely by surprise when his lips brushed lightly over hers. Whatever she had expected, it was not this. She stood transfixed, a mixture of horror and excitement muddling through her mind.

Then common sense prevailed and she raised her hands to push him off. But he caught her wrists, holding them back against the wall, moving closer so that their bodies touched, at the same time shutting the door with his heel.

'Let me go!' she slung furiously at him.

'When I'm good and ready.' His voice was low and sensual, and she felt his tautened muscles against her; she felt every bone and sinew in his hard body. 'I want to prove to you, Lucy, that I'm not at all the type of man you've labelled me.'

'And I'll prove to you that I don't like men who take advantage,' she muttered, aiming her toe at his shin.

He did not flinch, but his grip tightened until it felt as though her wrists were bound by bands of steel. 'You brute!' she hissed, wresting her head from side to side to avoid his looming mouth. 'Just wait till my mother hears about *this*. I bet she has no idea what sort of a monster you are.' Her green eyes glittered with fury.

'You're beautiful,' he breathed, and his mouth closed on hers with unerring accuracy. It was a kiss like no other, and an unconscious moan escaped Lucy's throat as he forced her clamped lips apart, beginning an exploration which ravaged her senses. It lasted for ever, and when he finally let her go she struggled for breath.

Nor was he finished with her. He trailed his fingertips over her face, observing her over-bright eyes, the trembling of her lips, the pulse beating erratically in her throat. She looked at him and there was hunger in his eyes. Lucy felt limp and hypnotised, and wondered how she could stand here and let him touch her.

But when he nudged aside the silky material of her blouse to kiss the soft mounds of her breasts, and when his fingers began to undo the buttons, she knew that enough was enough. This was insanity, madness. A shudder racked through her. 'Don't,' she whispered, agonised. 'Let me go, please.'

A slow smile curved his lips. 'I've made a strong enough impression?'

She hung her head in shame. How could she have stood there and let him kiss her? How could she?

'You took what you wanted,' she said quietly.

He put a finger to her chin. 'Are you denying that you enjoyed it?'

A tremor raced through Lucy's slender frame as her eyes met his. 'It was an experience.'

He smiled slowly. 'And one I would like to repeat.'

'There's no chance of that,' she rasped, whirling suddenly away from him. 'You're forgetting one tiny thing. I hate you with every fibre of my being. Now, will you please go?'

'How the lady changes,' he mocked. 'A few seconds ago, you were putty in my arms. It promises to be a tempestuous relationship. Goodbye for now, my spirited friend. I'm really looking forward to the next time we meet.'

## CHAPTER TWO

LUCY slammed the door furiously behind Conan. That had been a mistake, a big mistake. She ought never to have let him kiss her.

She leaned back against the wall, closing her eyes, listening to the sound of the Porsche as it sprang into life. It was a powerful car; he was a powerful man. Not just physically, although that as well. But his whole personality was so much greater, so much more dominant than that of any other man she had met. He had an air about him that came with success. He was totally confident, knew what he wanted and how to get it.

*Damn!* Why had she let him kiss her? She had given him a finger-hold. She had let him see that beneath her hostility she was as vulnerable as any other girl. But at least she now knew the strength of him, she knew what she was up against, and she would make very sure that nothing like it happened again.

Heaving a sigh, Lucy walked slowly upstairs. 'Have I made an impression?' That was what he had said to her. 'A strong enough impression?' He had done that the day he took her father to court. She had known then what a ruthless man he was. Now she had seen his ruthlessness in another guise.

She hung away her suit, pushing it distastefully to the back of her wardrobe, stripped off the rest of her clothes and stood beneath the shower.

Lucy was not very tall, about five-four, and she was slender and well-proportioned, although personally she thought that her breasts were too large. No one else did. Some of her flatter-chested friends envied her, even.

As she soaped herself now she could not help thinking how close Conan had come to suckling her breasts. She had looked down and seen his dark head against her, and for an insane moment had actually enjoyed the rasp of his lips and tongue against her soft skin.

Oh, God, it was lunacy! What was she doing, letting this man intrude into her thoughts? Savagely she turned the shower to cold, and stood and let it drench her until she was shivering from head to toe. But at least it had the desired effect. She no longer felt vulnerable; her trembling awareness had gone. All she wanted to do was slip into something casual and forget about Conan Templeton.

And she thought she had succeeded. She was actually humming a tune to herself when she went back downstairs, but in the lounge were their teacups, and memories quickly returned. With compressed lips Lucy took the tray through to the kitchen and rinsed the cups under the tap, then went out into the garden. The evening air was warm, sparrows chattered in a nearby elm, and the scent of honeysuckle hung heavy in the air. Her mother couldn't have picked a nicer day to get married. June wasn't always a kind month.

Absently she sat down on the bench her father had built, thinking about the events that had led up to his death. Her mother had never told her that he had a heart condition. The shock of discovering that his best friend had swindled him must have hurt dreadfully. And he must have known he would not live through all the trauma of the court case, because he had left her mother a letter saying how upset he was, and how worried, and how much he loved her. He said he felt sure the blame was his, that he had not been paying Martin enough money, and how sorry he felt for the man, having an invalid wife.

Eric Anderson had had his fatal heart attack at the wheel of his car the day after the court case. Fortunately there had been no other traffic on the road when he crashed.

It did Lucy good, reviving these memories. It made her realise what a hateful man Conan Templeton really was. It was his fault her father had died, his and no one else's, and she must be insane agreeing to work for him.

She lay awake for a long time that night, tormented by thoughts of this man. She really could not understand her mother's forgiving the Templetons. If it hadn't been for them her husband would still be alive.

Finally she fell into a deep sleep and was awakened by the telephone shrilling downstairs. It took Lucy a second or two to remember that she was back home and that her mother had got married and she was the only person in the house.

Her eyes were still half closed as she groped her way downstairs. She hoped it wasn't Conan Templeton making a nuisance of himself again.

'Hi, Lucy, it's Mike. Mike Ridding. I heard you were back.'

Lucy smiled her relief. 'Oh, hello, Mike. How are you?' Mike was one of the crowd she used to knock around with before she went to college. Most of them were engaged or married by now, but she had heard at the reception yesterday that Mike was still single and without a steady girlfriend.

'I'm fine. How about you? You sound as though I've got you out of bed.'

'You have,' she grimaced, rubbing sleepily at her eyes. 'What time is it?'

'Just turned eleven.'

'Heavens! Is it really?' What had made her sleep in so long?

'How would you like to go out to lunch? All sorts of things have been happening. I have lots to tell you.'

'I'm sorry, Mike,' said Lucy, visualising his disappointment. 'It's good to hear from you, but the house looks like a bomb's hit it and I start a new job tomorrow, so I must get it straight. Thanks all the same.'

'A job, eh? How did you manage that so quickly?'

'My mother fixed it for me.'

'Lucky you.'

Hardly lucky, she thought.

'So when can I see you? Tomorrow night?'

'I don't think so,' she replied. 'It's my first ever job, don't forget. I'll probably be worn out.' If the work didn't do it, sparring with Conan would. She was definitely not looking forward to tomorrow.

'Is this a put-off?' Mike complained, but she could hear the smile in his voice. They had always been good friends, and she knew she could say what she liked without hurting his feelings. She had been out with him on occasions, but they had never dated seriously.

'Let me ring you,' she said.

'But you won't,' he groaned. 'You're forgetting, I know what you're like. I'll phone you again towards the end of the week, and next time I won't take no for an answer.'

'OK, Mike,' she smiled. 'Thanks for ringing, anyway.'

'Where's the job, by the way?'

'C.T. Steels, personal secretary to Conan Templeton. He's actually my new stepbrother.'

There was silence for a moment. 'What's he like?'

She grinned into the phone. 'Mike Ridding, I do believe you're jealous. He's tall, dark and handsome, and very rich.'

'I see,' he said, a thoughtful tone entering his voice. 'No wonder you don't want to come out with me.'

She giggled into the phone. 'There's one thing about him that you might like to hear.'

'And that is?'

'I hate his guts.'

Another pause, silent shock at the vehemence in her tone, then, 'I don't understand. Why work for a guy you don't like?'

'I can't disappoint my mother. I'll give it a go. If it doesn't work out I can always leave.'

'May I ask why you don't like him?'

Lucy could hear the puzzlement in Mike's voice. 'You may, but I'm not going to tell you, not now. Maybe some time.'

'Like the next time I see you?'

'Perhaps.'

'I care about you, Lucy, you know that. I don't want you to get hurt.'

'I won't, Mike. Thanks for ringing. 'Bye.'

Mike was a good friend. There was nothing between them romantically, and there never would be; he was more like a brother. But he did concern himself about her wellbeing, and for that she was grateful. She might need him in the days to come.

Lucy spent the day cleaning and tidying, managing to sun herself in the garden for a while, congratulating herself, when she finally went to bed, on pushing Conan Templeton firmly out of her mind.

But although she had not consciously thought about him, her subconscious was a different matter. In her dreams his lovemaking was even more devastating than it had been in reality. Lucy woke hot and bothered and took a long, cooling shower before dressing carefully in an uncrushable off-white dress with a pleated skirt. Damn Conan! Why was he doing this to her?

Breakfast was nothing more than a hasty slice of toast and a cup of coffee, and a feeling of foreboding stole over Lucy as she nosed her car out of the garage and into the maniacal rush-hour traffic.

Derby, where C.T. Steels had its offices, was no more than twelve miles away, but it took her almost an hour to get there and she was late.

Conan Templeton's face was dark wth anger when she finally found her way to his office suite on the top floor of a lavish new building. Lucy could not help thinking that her father's money had gone towards this. Consequently she was as angry as he when they came face to face. It had been a mistake, a big mistake coming here. She ought never to have let him goad her.

'What time do you call this?' He shot back a white cuff to glance at his slim gold watch.

Lucy's chin jerked and she eyed him with dislike. 'I got held up in the traffic.' He wore a grey pin-striped suit this morning, and a white shirt and maroon tie. He looked devastating, and she hated him.

'Then you should have allowed more time.'

With difficulty Lucy held back an angry retort. 'I will in future.' There was no point beginning the day with an unholy row. It looked like being bad enough.

'See that you do. Bad timekeeping is one thing I will not allow.'

Lucy wondered how he treated his other employees. It was sometimes impossible to avoid being late. Did he listen to their excuses, or dismiss them?

'This is your office, and mine is through there. The mail's on your desk. When you've sorted it out, bring it in to me.'

He spoke peremptorily and hardly gave her a further glance as he strode through into his own domain. A complete contrast to the man who had kissed her so unexpectedly. And she was glad. This she could cope with.

They had told her at college that bosses were sometimes rude and inconsiderate, that they expected perfection and could not tolerate inefficiency. That a secretary was expected to anticipate her boss's needs and show no aggression or resentment if he chose to berate her—which he was quite likely to do until she had proved herself. Not all bosses were the same, some were understanding and kindness itself. But she had known Conan Templeton would not fall into this category. No man who could cold-bloodedly take someone to court for money he did not possess could possibly have an ounce of kindness in him.

She glanced around her room. It held the latest in high technology, and she hoped he would give her time to familiarise herself with the equipment. She wondered why his other secretary had left before a replacement was found. Perhaps a clash of personalities? Perhaps this girl too had felt the cutting edge of his tongue?

Lucy mentally squared her shoulders. She was not easily put down. She would do her best, and if she felt he was criticising her unjustly she would defend herself. She slit open the envelopes and took the mail through. He had taken off his jacket and loosened his tie, and looked ready to do business.

'I'll have a cup of coffee,' he said. 'Strong and black with no sugar. I have another at eleven and one mid-afternoon if I'm in. You'll find all you need in the kitch-enette off your office.'

Lucy nodded.

'And when you've made that, bring your notebook in.'

She made two cups of coffee, put one on her desk and took Conan's through to him. She never drank it. He dictated solidly for over an hour, letter after letter, memo after memo. She had groaned and grumbled at college when she had been pushed to write shorthand at a hundred and forty words a minute, but now she was glad. It still took all her concentration.

By the time he had finished her neck and shoulders were aching and the cup of coffee on her desk was covered with a revolting skin. She poured it down the sink and drank a glass of water instead, then applied herself to the task of typing out Conan's letters.

The morning fled. She took phone calls and made his coffee, made three more cups when he had visitors, booked him a table for lunch, and managed to find her way through the filing system when he asked for infor-mation on a customer.

When he left the office she leaned back in her chair and closed her eyes. He had kept her so busy all morning that every ounce of energy had drained out of her. And she was not half-way through his letters!

A tap on the door heralded a pretty redhead who in-troduced herself as Jo, declaring that she was secretary to Bob Swift, the Sales Director. Her office was next door.

'How're you doing?' she grinned, dropping into a chair. 'A bit of a slave-driver, is our revered Mr Templeton.'

'You're telling me. How long since his last secretary left? There's so much work it's unbelievable.'

'Viva?' grinned Jo. 'A week, that's all.'

'Couldn't she have waited until Conan found someone else?'

The other girl's brows rose. 'You're on first-name terms already? I always——'

Lucy checked her with a laugh. 'He's my stepbrother.'

'I see,' said Jo. 'We all wondered how he'd found someone permanent so quickly. He usually has to rely on temps in these circumstances.'

'Meaning his secretaries walk out on him often?' It made sense.

'Not in the least,' Jo surprised her. 'He works them hard, but the rewards are good too.'

'Like dinner out with the boss and bed afterwards?'

Jo's eyes widened at Lucy's cynicism. 'Something tells me you don't very much like your stepbrother?'

Lucy shrugged. 'We've only just met, actually. I finished college last week and my mother fixed this job up for me. But let's say that so far I'm not enamoured.'

'Now, that does surprise me,' said Jo. 'Most girls, in fact, I would go so far as to say *all* girls, fall head over heels in love with our Mr Templeton. One of the reasons he gets rid of them. They become an embarrassment. It's not he who does the chasing, you understand.'

So why had he kissed her? The thought circled in Lucy's mind. But it remained a puzzle. One thing was certain, however: she would never chase him. 'So what sort of rewards are you talking about?'

'Monetary ones,' answered Jo at once. 'High salaries, overtime, private medical care, Christmas parties, summer suppers. We're one big happy family, unless you abuse the favours you're granted, then you're out on your ear. Most people, though, have been here for years and years. I've been here ten myself.'

'Are you married?'

Jo nodded. 'I have a little girl, but we have a crèche here and a resident nanny. Who could ask for more? And of course he gets the best out of his workers, treating them as he does.'

This did not sound like the Conan Templeton that Lucy knew, and she frowned.

'Anyway, I've come to see if you'd like to join me for lunch. The prices in the dining-room are most reasonable. I usually have ten minutes with Amy before she goes to sleep and then the rest of my lunch-hour is my own.'

'I've brought sandwiches,' admitted Lucy. 'I had no idea.'

'Seems to me that your stepbrother hasn't told you very much at all. How come you've only just met?'

'I've been living in London. I actually only met my stepfather on Saturday as well.'

'Alan Templeton? He's nice, too. We heard he was getting married. So in actual fact, you're now part of the company?' Jo looked impressed.

'I wouldn't say that,' said Lucy quickly. 'My mother maybe, but not me. I don't particularly want to associate myself with the Templetons.' As soon as the words were out, Lucy regretted them. 'Thanks for the offer of lunch,' she went on hurriedly, 'but I think I'll eat my sandwiches here and try and get on with this work while Conan's out.'

Jo grimaced. 'That's what I call being keen. Tomorrow, maybe?'

'Tomorrow,' agreed Lucy with a faint smile.

And when Conan came back from lunch with a lengthy schedule he wanted doing on the word processor, Lucy was glad she had caught up with her work.

All in all, it was a relief when the day ended. Lucy was mentally and physically exhausted, and could imagine nothing nicer than a long, hot soak in the bath and an early night.

There followed a week of punishing days, when Conan drove her to the limits of her capabilities, and she had no idea whether he was pleased with her or not. She made mistakes to begin with and she had to ask lots of questions because it was all so new and strange to her, but soon she learned the routine and understood the computer and felt that she was doing quite well.

When Mike rang she told him she was too tired to go out, maybe at the weekend, and then on Friday Conan informed Lucy that he wanted her in the office the next morning.

Lucy had been so looking forward to a lazy day, perhaps lying in bed for an extra hour or two, that she pulled a face. 'I didn't realise I was expected to work on Saturdays.'

His eyes narrowed at her unenthusiastic response. 'My secretary works whenever I need her.'

Jo had already told Lucy that she was lucky Mr Templeton had not asked her to work late, that he sometimes kept his secretary busy until six and seven at night. 'It must be because you're a relative,' grinned the redhead.

'That probably works against me rather than for me,' retorted Lucy. She had still not told Jo the real reason she didn't like Conan, nor did she intend to. Lucy had discovered that the other girl was an inveterate gossip, and anything she said was swiftly common knowledge.

'I'm not saying I won't do it,' she said to Conan now. 'It's just that it was unexpected.'

'Good,' he crisped. 'Come in at eight and maybe you'll get away before lunch.' And that was the end to the conversation. Lucy was not very happy.

The next morning her alarm failed, and at eight o'clock she was still in bed. The phone shrilled downstairs, and when she reached it Conan's angry voice boomed in her ear. 'What's going on?'

Lucy was instantly wide awake. 'I overslept. My alarm never went off. I'm sorry. I'm coming now.'

She leapt up the stairs, splashed her face with cold water, threw on her clothes and was out of the door in five minutes flat. It was not until she was impatiently cursing the traffic that she asked herself why she was rushing, why she was letting him bother her like this. She hated the guy, didn't she? So why run at his bidding? The answer escaped her.

He was pacing up and down like a caged lion. There were two tapes on her desk which he had presumably dictated while waiting. He normally hated using the dictaphone, much preferring to dictate to her directly, but he also hated wasting time. Lucy had already discovered that.

He was never idle for one moment. He had his finger on every pulse in the business. Through the computer in his office he could tell at the touch of a button what the stock position was at any one of his companies, what their finances were like, what orders were on the books, whether there was any problem in despatching them, what sort of prices their competitors were quoting. Everything. It was all there.

But he did not sit and stare at the green screen all day. He had daily meetings with his managers and directors, where Lucy was expected to take notes. Everything was recorded. Nothing was left open to contradiction at a later date. He spent part of his time on the shop-floor, and knew the name personally of each of his employees, even down to the cleaning ladies, and he always had time for a few words with them. How were they getting on? Had they any problems, any complaints? He was well-liked and respected, and treated everyone fairly.

On the other hand he was not soft. Lucy heard him on the telephone when he was trying to arrange a deal; she sat in on meetings and listened to him arguing terms. And almost always he got his own way. Bills were settled promptly, taking advantage of discounts, and he expected his customers to pay him on time too. She now understood why he had come down so hard on her father. But she did not agree with it. There were such things as extenuating circumstances. Didn't he ever take those into account? Was his sole concern making money?

He saw her eyeing the tapes. 'I'd like those done straight away.'

Instead of his formal business suit, he wore pale blue polished satin trousers this morning and a half-sleeved blue and white shirt. On his feet were soft blue leather shoes and his black hair was freshly shampooed, his jaw clean-shaven. He smelt of something woody and intoxicating, and in contrast Lucy felt decidedly scruffy in the same grey skirt and blouse as yesterday. She had not bothered with make-up, and a gust of wind as she stepped out of the car had dishevelled her hair.

But she dared not spend time on her appearance. He was returning to his office, but his anger was apparent in the straight lines of his back. Lucy gave a mental shrug and plugged in her machine, slotting in the cassette and putting on her earphones.

Conan's voice sounded different. He had a deep voice anyway, but on the tape it was even deeper, with a resonance to it and a disturbingly sensual element. She found herself listening to him with her eyes closed instead of getting on with the job of keying the report into the word processor. It amazed her that she found his voice attractive when she hated the man himself so intensely.

'Is there something you can't understand?'

Lucy jumped and turned startled wide eyes in his direction. 'Not really.' He had come in so quietly that she had not heard him. His anger seemed to have gone, and there was a quirk at the corner of his mouth that was suspiciously like a smile.

'Then I suggest you get on with it, or we'll be here all day.'

Lucy obediently resumed her task, and this time she did not allow herself to get carried away by his hypnotic voice.

Once finished, Lucy printed out the report and took a copy into him. He was sitting back in his chair staring into space. It was so unusual for him to be doing nothing that Lucy wondered if something was wrong. 'Sit down, Lucy,' he said.

She sat, pulling her skirt demurely over her knees, aware that he was looking at her with something more than the indifference he had shown over the last week.

Following the kiss he had given her the day of her mother's wedding, Lucy had fully expected to have to fight off his advances. Instead Conan ignored her altogether on a personal level. All he had been interested in was her ability to do his work and do it well.

'I think maybe the least I can do,' he said, 'is take you out to lunch.'

Lucy eyed him guardedly. 'No, thanks. If those tapes were all you wanted, then if you don't mind I'll go.'

She made to stand but he stopped her with a gesture. 'Why not? You have to eat.'

'But not with you. You know how I feel. My mother might have forgiven you Templetons, but I never will. I'll do my job, but that's as far as it goes.'

'And may I say that you're a credit to the college. I must admit I had my reservations about employing someone without actual experience.'

'Then why did you?' she questioned sharply.

'Your mother persuaded me it would be in my best interests.'

'I don't believe that. I've seen what you're like. They told us about your type at college, demanding and expecting efficiency. All hell to pay if you don't get it. You wouldn't take a risk.'

His lips twisted. 'Why not? You're a beautiful girl, Lucy.'

'You'd never met me. How did you know what I was like?'

'Believe me, I knew.'

As she had known him! Lucy clenched her teeth and glared. 'Beautiful girls don't always make the best secretaries.'

'Yes, I know,' he said.

'And my mother must have told you what my feelings were about the man who took my father to court.'

'I enjoy a challenge,' he mocked easily, his gaze flickering over her, his eyes black and smoky and sensual. It was difficult to ignore their message.

Lucy was conscious that they were the only two in the building. She was in a very perilous situation. 'It will be a long, hard battle if you think you're ever going to get through to me,' she said tightly.

He stood up and walked round the desk, standing behind her and over her, brushing a finger against her cheek. 'I think I've already started.' His tone was soft and insinuating, and Lucy knew that he was referring to her unwitting response the other night. But it would never happen again, she would make sure of that.

She desperately wanted to knock his hand away, to scream at him not to touch her, but she refused to give him the pleasure of knowing what sensations he aroused. They were insanity and best ignored. Instead she very carefully stood up, and her voice was ice-cold when she said, 'Do you make a habit of this sort of thing, Mr Templeton?'

'It depends how badly I want something.'

It had been a mistake, standing and facing him, Lucy realised it now. His smoky eyes had darkened and he touched her face again, this time outlining her lips with a gentle fingertip, all the time watching closely for her reaction.

'And you badly want to take me to lunch, is that it?'

'Not so much as I'd like to make love to you.'

Lucy gasped her disbelief and would have shot away had he not slid his arms around her and pulled her to him. She could feel the hardness of his body, his chest and thighs moulded against hers, and she felt vulnerable again, and uneasy, and knew that, if he should try to force himself on her, her strength was pitifully weak compared to his.

She flashed her green eyes. 'Do you know what you're doing? Making me hate you all the more.'

'I don't think so.' His tone was deep and meaningful. 'You might have control of your mind, Lucy. You might tell yourself you hate me. You might indeed hate me. But your body speaks a different story.'

'And is that all you're after?' she demanded, pushing her hands fiercely against him. But all she succeeded in doing was welding the lower half of them even more firmly together. And there was no ignoring his arousal.

'Your body? No.' With an amused smile he let her go. 'Strange as it may seem, I want more from you than that.'

'You could have fooled me,' she snapped. 'Jo said it's usually your secretaries who chase you. I think she must have got it the wrong way round.'

He grimaced ruefully. 'No, she's right.'

'Then why am I singled out for this—this special treatment?'

'Because—you're a special girl.'

'In what way? Are you trying to make up somehow because you killed my father?'

His mouth firmed and a pulse jerked in his jaw. 'Don't say we're back on that again.'

'You expect me to forget it?' she demanded.

'It's been two years since your father died,' he thrust impatiently. 'Can't you forget who I am and what happened?'

Her eyes flashed. 'My father was forty-nine. What sort of an age do you think that is to die? He was in his prime, he loved his life, his work, everything.'

'They're like chips of emeralds.'

Lucy frowned. 'What are?'

'Your eyes when you're angry.'

She drew a deep, impatient breath. 'Are you listening to one word I say?'

'Oh, yes, I'm listening.'

'Then you agree it was tragic for my father to die so young?'

'Of course I agree, but it wasn't my fault, Lucy. According to your mother, he already had a heart condition. Anything could have triggered it off.'

'Like being taken to court,' she rasped.

He shrugged. 'It could have been the shock of finding his partner and old friend had embezzled him. Maybe it's Martin Goodfellow you should be directing your hate-campaign against?'

'If I knew where Martin was,' she spat, 'I'd certainly make sure he knows how I feel. He started it all, I'll admit that, but you were the one who drove the nail in my father's coffin.'

His head jerked at her strong words. 'I refuse to accept that, Lucy. It was not a personal vendetta.'

'But you showed no lenience.'

'Your father's firm was not the first to owe me money, and I doubt he'll be the last. I'm not a charity, Lucy, I'm a businessman, and if I have to take someone to court to get what's mine by rights, then that's what I do.'

'You're a swine.'

'And you're illogical. Use your common sense.'

Lucy closed her eyes to shut out the vision of this darkly attractive but hateful man. 'Where you're concerned I have none. I know what happened and that's all I'm interested in. Not why, now how, not because.

You can go on giving me excuses until Doomsday. Facts are facts, and you can't get away from them.'

He stepped back from her, his face tight now, his good humour gone. His eyes were hard and cold and pierced right through her. 'Do you know what I ought to do, Lucy Anderson? I ought to put you over my knee and give you the good hiding you deserve. They might have taught you office procedure at college, but they certainly never taught you good manners.'

'I can't say I think much of your behaviour, either,' she riposted.

He laughed suddenly and caught her wrists, and the next second his mouth was on hers, and Lucy felt every vein and every nerve ignite. Sparring with him had heightened her awareness, but she was totally unprepared for this surge of sensation.

His first kiss had caught her unawares, had drawn an unexpected response, but this was something else. It was as though the taste of him had whetted her appetite and now she hungered for more. But it was lunacy. How could you hate a man with every breath and yet crave his body?

But whatever thoughts warred through her mind, her lips parted, and his kiss deepened, and Lucy felt as though he were drugging her senses. Everything else faded, and as the aggression died out of her his grip relaxed and his hands began a slow, seductive massage over her back.

Subconsciously she pressed herself against him, her own hands sliding up into the exciting thickness of his hair, exploring the shape of his head, drinking from his mouth and savouring every second.

'That's better.' His mouth was close to her ear now, his breath warm on her cheek. Lucy had her eyes closed and she could feel her heart pounding erratically.

His tongue probed the intricate curves of her ear, he nibbled her lobe and trailed kisses back towards her mouth. When he suddenly let her go Lucy felt bereft.

'Have you changed your mind about lunch?' he asked quietly.

'No.' Almost she had said yes. Almost. It had trembled on the tip of her tongue. But sanity was taking over. Free at last from his stimulating embrace, she could think clearly.

'*No!* What you've just done makes me hate you even more. You're despicable, Conan Templeton.'

'Maybe that's what you think at this moment, my lovely Lucy. But one day you're going to change your mind. Make no mistake about that. One day you're going to feel quite differently about me. And hopefully I won't have to wait too long.'

# CHAPTER THREE

ON MONDAY morning Lucy dressed carefully in a straight cream skirt and navy blouse and wondered what sort of a day it was going to be. She was not looking forward to it. Would Conan be the impersonal boss or the amorous lover?

Her whole weekend had been spent in a state of confusion. She hated Conan, and she hated herself for letting him get through to her. If only she knew what he was trying to prove, why he was doing this to her. It was a game, surely? He wasn't really interested, not in a sexual way, not in any other way. Perhaps it was because of her professed hatred; it amused him to try and change her opinion of him? But she would never, in the whole of her life, forgive him for what he had done to her father.

She need not have worried, Conan was not there. He was in Sheffield. He had left a note on her desk stating that would be back tomorrow night, a pile of letters for her to answer, and a list of instructions to follow.

It was something of an anticlimax to find that she had the office to herself, but it was also beautiful not to have his powerful presence hanging over her. She was still very busy, but there was none of that urgency and desperation, and now she knew her way around she took time to chat to some of the other secretaries, who all envied her working for their devilishly handsome chairman.

Jo was still trying to worm out of her why she did not like Conan Templeton, but Lucy gave nothing away. She

43

had got into the habit of lunching in the dining-room with Jo and another girl and, despite her initial misgivings, Lucy decided that she was enjoying her job.

On Tuesday afternoon she found herself with a quiet moment and phoned Mike. He was delighted to hear from her. 'How about that meal?' she asked him pertly.

'Lovely. When? Tonight?'

'If that's OK?'

'OK? It's the best offer I've had for a week. My parents are away and I've been cooking for myself. It's not much fun, I assure you.'

Lucy grinned into the phone. 'Pick me up about eight. We'll go to Torrelino's, they always give you plenty.'

And so it was arranged. Lucy decided to wear a silky two-piece with flame-red poppies on a pale green background, teamed with the green bag and shoes she had bought for the wedding. Mike was impressed. 'All this for me?'

Lucy closed the front door and followed him out to his car. 'Who else?' she asked mischievously.

Mike was a couple of inches taller than Lucy, with sandy hair and twinkling blue eyes. 'I thought you might have been seeing something of your new stepbrother?' It was a light-hearted question, but Lucy guessed he was more serious than he sounded.

'Have you forgotten that I hate him?'

'No.' He opened the car door for her. 'But you've had a week to change your mind.'

Lucy smiled cynically. 'I never will.'

During their meal he asked her how she was getting on with her job.

Lucy grimaced. 'I found it frightening at first, there was so much to remember and do, and Conan's not the most patient of men, but now I'm settling in and actually enjoying it.'

'Despite how you feel?'

She nodded.

'Is it mutual? Does he dislike you?'

Lucy shook her head with a vague frown. 'I don't really know.' And that was the truth.

'But he's not too hard on you, he's not making your life unbearable?'

A faint smile curved Lucy's lips. Far from it. Unless you called being kissed unbearable? 'No. He can't stand incompetence, but I have to reluctantly admit that he's very fair. The staff all seem to like and respect him, and the business is run like a well-oiled machine.'

'So, what's the feud about? Are you going to tell me?'

Lucy swallowed. There was no reason why she shouldn't. He was her friend, after all. 'You remember the trouble my father had before he died?'

Mike nodded.

'Well, it was Conan who took him to court.' Lucy straightened in her seat and her tone hardened, her eyes suddenly blazing with hatred. *Conan effectively killed my father.'*

'Lucy!' Mike was shocked by the abrupt change in her.

'It's true, he did,' she defended.

'Not intentionally.'

'As good as. I'll never forgive him.'

'I see. It must make life difficult. Why did you take the job?'

Her chin lifted. 'It was a matter of pride. I'd already said I'd do it before I realised who he was. But it's all right, we've reached an understanding. We don't let our personal feelings interfere with our work, and as I don't see him outside office hours it's no problem.'

Mike was thoughtful for a moment. 'How about your mother?'

She lifted her shoulders in defeat, her lips twisting wryly. 'To my amazement, what happened has made no difference. She loves Alan and that's all there is to it. I can't understand her.'

'Maybe she's wiser than you think.'

Lucy eyed him disdainfully. 'Don't you start that. Conan seems to think I should emulate her as well. But I can't. I *can't*.' She closed her eyes and said more quietly, 'You've no idea what it was like, knowing that I'd never be able to talk to my father again. He was so wise and so kind and I loved him so much, and no matter what anyone says, I shall always blame Conan.'

There was a break in her voice and Mike touched her hand across the table. 'I'm sorry, Lucy.'

With difficulty she swallowed the tight lump in her throat. 'It's me who should apologise for going on like this. Would you mind very much if we left? I don't think I can eat any more.'

'Of course.' Mike paid the bill and they went out to his car, a dark blue Escort with a very new scratch along one side. No comparison to the Porsche, thought Lucy idly, and yet, settled in her seat, she felt far more comfortable.

Mike drove her straight home. 'Would you like me to come in?' he asked diffidently.

And although Lucy wanted to be alone, she felt guilty because she had cut short his evening, so she nodded and he followed her inside.

'I'm going to change,' she said. 'I won't be a moment. Make yourself at home. There's a beer in the fridge.'

The phone rang as she stood in her undies hanging her suit away. 'Get that, Mike, will you, please?' she called. 'Tell whoever it is that I'll ring them back.'

When she went downstairs he informed her that it had been Conan Templeton.

Lucy frowned. 'What did he want? Was he ringing from Sheffield?' Conan was the last person she felt like speaking to at this moment.

'He didn't say. He seemed a bit taken aback, hearing a man's voice. Asked me who I was and what I was doing here.'

'I hope you told him to mind his own business?' she flashed.

Mike smiled. 'I told him I was a friend, a close friend, and he went very quiet and rang off.'

'Good.' Lucy's fingers were strumming unconsciously on the edge of the table.

'What you need is a good strong drink,' said Mike. 'You shouldn't let him get through to you.'

'How can I help it?' she grated. 'But I'll have a whisky, please—neat.'

After two drinks she felt calmer and Mike left. She went to bed but not to sleep. In the far west there were still pale streaks of light in the sky, and she watched until they were no more. But it was still several hours before she slept.

There were shadows beneath her eyes the next morning. Conan had returned from Sheffield and was sitting at his desk. He frowned when she took in his mail. 'A late night?'

She jutted her chin. 'What's it to do with you?'

'I promised your mother I'd keep an eye on you.'

Lucy gasped, even though she could quite believe it. Probably her mother had asked him. But, despite what they both might think, she was perfectly capable of looking after herself. 'I don't need anyone to check up on me,' she said tightly. 'I've lived alone for the last two years without any problems.'

'Who's Mike Ridding?'

She eyed him coldly. 'A friend.'

'What sort of a friend?'

'The best there is.'

'Did he stay the night?'

'You have a nerve!' she snapped. 'My private life's my own affair.'

'You haven't answered my question.' His black eyes were level on hers.

'And I don't intend to. Is that all, Mr Templeton?'

A muscle jerked in his jaw. 'For the moment.'

She turned and left, feeling his eyes on her, feeling also a certain smug satisfaction that she had given him food for thought. But at least if he believed she had a boyfriend he might think again before trying to kiss her.

She made his coffee and took it in while he was on the phone. She could not help overhearing the conversation. He was talking to their Accounts Manager. 'I don't care what sort of promises he's made. He's never kept them before. Put it in the hands of our solicitor.'

Lucy went cold all over. It was happening again, to some other poor, unfortunate man. She retreated to her office and sat down, cupping her hands round her cup, trying to draw some warmth from it. The intercom buzzed. 'Lucy, bring your notebook in.'

How was she going to keep the hatred out of her face? She had bragged to Mike that they never allowed personal gripes to enter their business relationship, but in the light of what she had just heard it would be impossible.

She picked up her pad and pencil and made her way reluctantly through to Conan's office. It was a much bigger room than her own, elegantly fitted out with Scandinavian furniture and an almost white carpet. Normally it had a calming influence on her, but this morning it felt like a death cell.

'Is something wrong?' He observed her pallor and the cold numbness in her eyes. 'You didn't look too good when you came in, but now you look worse. Are you ill?'

Lucy swallowed and shook her head.

Conan frowned. 'Then what is it?'

'Just thoughts.'

A slight pause, then, 'Me?'

'Who else?'

His frown deepened.

'But I don't want to talk about it,' she added quickly. She opened her pad and sat down with it on her knee. 'Let's get on.'

He did not argue, but all the time he was dictating, Lucy was conscious of his gaze on her, and when he had finished he crossed to his drinks cupboard and poured her a glass of brandy. He didn't say anything, he just handed it to her and she took it and sipped it and began to feel better, though nothing, she guessed, would ever melt the ice-cold hatred packed around her heart.

When the glass was empty she stood up and left the room, and began to automatically transcribe her shorthand on to the typewriter.

At eleven she made more coffee, taking his silently into him, then returning to resume her work. He had an appointment at twelve, and as he passed through her office with his briefcase in his hand he paused. 'Take the afternoon off, Lucy.'

There was kindness in his tone which grated on her nerves. All a face. He wasn't like this at all, he was cold and hard and unfeeling, and she wanted to walk out of here and never come back. But that would be admitting defeat. She could cope. *She could*. Lucy straightened her back. 'It's all right, I can do my work.'

His brows shrugged. 'If that's how you feel. I should be back about four. If not, sign my mail for me.'

When he had gone Lucy put her head in her hands and sat for a few minutes. Then she got up and took some aspirins and decided to have an early lunch. She would go for a walk, get some much-needed fresh air, get right away from the sudden cloying atmosphere of the office.

Conan never came back. Lucy went home at five, and there was a card on the hall floor from her mother, which cheered her somewhat. She and Alan were thoroughly enjoying themselves. Lucy wished she could be as forgiving as her parent, but her nature was totally different and it was impossible.

Mike phoned and asked whether he could come round, and Lucy agreed. She needed someone to cheer her up. But he had been there for no more than a few minutes when Conan's car pulled up outside. Lucy saw it through the window and groaned.

'Conan Templeton?' guessed Mike correctly.

She nodded.

'Do you want me to get rid of him?'

'It doesn't matter, I'll see what he wants.' Lucy went to the door and opened it, but she did not step back for him to enter.

'How are you feeling?'

'Much better, thank you,' she said coldly.

'I see you have company.' He glanced at the navy car.

'That's right.'

'Your boyfriend?'

'It's Mike, yes.'

'In which case I'm wasting my time. I seem to have called unnecessarily. Goodbye, Lucy.' Without another word he turned and left. Lucy could not accept that he had called simply to see how she was. What could it matter to him?

She gave a mental shrug and closed the door. 'What did he want?' asked Mike.

'A good question. I've really no idea. He asked me how I was and who was here, and then left.'

Mike's sandy brows rose. 'Is that all?'

Lucy nodded.

'Perhaps he would have invited himself in if I hadn't been here?'

'Then it's as well you are, because he's not welcome,' Lucy said sharply.

Mike pulled a wry face. 'You really do have it in for him, don't you?'

'Wouldn't you, under the same circumstances?' she shot back.

'Maybe,' said Mike quietly.

Lucy shook her head angrily. 'Let's not talk about him any more.' But the evening was ruined, she couldn't get Conan out of her mind, and Mike left early.

The next morning Lucy woke with a thumping headache and felt tempted to take the day off. But it was an excuse and she knew it, and that was unlike her. She always faced up to things, no matter how unpleasant.

She took more time than usual over her make-up and put on a soft pearl-grey dress that always made her feel good. A last check in the mirror told her that she had convincingly hidden the pallor of her skin and the shadows beneath her eyes, but her hair was getting out of shape. She must have it cut.

Conan was already at the office. Lucy made his coffee and took it through to him with his mail. She felt him looking at her critically and her skin grew warm. He seemed not to miss one inch of her anatomy, from the tip of her painted toenails to the top of her shining black hair. It annoyed her that he had this ability to stir her senses, and she could not understand herself for responding so readily.

'Sit down, Lucy.'

She frowned, but obeyed. Normally he liked to be left alone at this time in a morning to read through his post.

'Now tell me what's wrong.'

'Nothing,' she said, avoiding his eyes.

'All that paint on your face is for nothing? It doesn't fool me. You hinted yesterday that I'm in some way to blame. If I am, then I think I have a right to know.'

'Isn't it obvious?' she scorned.

'Maybe I'm blind.'

'I just don't like the way you do business.'

A frown jagged Conan's brow. 'Elucidate.'

'You're going to take some other poor unfortunate to court.'

Conan frowned. 'I am? Who's told you that?'

'I couldn't help hearing you on the telephone to Mr Saul.'

'You heard me tell him to put it in the hands of our solicitors. A letter from them usually does the trick. It does not necessarily mean a court case.'

'But if the firm hasn't the money to pay?'

'Then the least they can do is write and tell us, instead of simply ignoring our requests. Businesses cannot be run on continual credit, you should know that.'

'Is that what my father did, ignored your requests?'

'Really, Lucy, I don't remember every individual case.'

'There are so many?'

'No, indeed. But I'm a very busy man. Jim Saul looks after that side of the business.'

'But you have the ultimate say?'

'Of course.'

'Then I still hold you responsible.'

He shook his head sadly. 'You're making a big mistake, Lucy. And the sooner you realise it, the happier you will be.'

'Is that all you want me for, to discuss my feelings?'

'They are of importance to me.'

She frowned. 'Why?'

'If you don't know, then I'm not going to tell you,' he answered quietly. 'How about letting me take you out to dinner tonight?'

His invitation was so unexpected that Lucy's head jerked. The pain made her wince.

'You have a headache?'

'I woke up with it,' she admitted, 'but I've taken some aspirin. It'll go.'

'If it's not gone by lunch time you'd best see the nurse. She can give you something stronger.'

'Stop fussing,' Lucy answered with some asperity. His concern was so false it was sickening.

'I'm merely being sensible. What's your answer?'

'I'll see how I feel.'

'I'm talking about dinner tonight.'

Lucy looked at him coolly. 'Why are you asking me?'

'Why does any man ask a beautiful girl? I'd like your company.'

'Or did my mother suggest you make sure I eat properly? Is that what this is all about?' Lucy's tone became sharp, her eyes scornful. 'It's all right, you know. I am looking after myself.'

Conan's mouth firmed. 'In more ways than one, yes, I've noticed. How much does this Mike fellow mean to you?'

'I've known him many years. We're very close.'

'Do you plan to marry him?'

'I think that's my business.'

'You're not engaged?'

'No,' answered Lucy warily.

'In that case I see no reason why you shouldn't come out with me.'

'Except that I don't want to.'

'You might be pleasantly surprised.'

'I've no doubt you can be very charming when you set out to be,' she derided, 'but I'm not interested. Not now, not ever.'

His eyes had never left her face during their discourse, but now they grew flint-like and his mouth tightened. 'I'm going to change your mind, Lucy, make no mistake about that.'

'What's wrong?' she challenged. 'Aren't you used to girls saying no? I'm different, am I? Is that what this is all about? It's a pity, isn't it? But never mind, I'm sure you'll find someone else to wine and dine and do whatever else you want to do to her.'

There was an acrimonious sweetness to her tone and his face darkened ominously, but when she stood up and swept out of his office he made no attempt to detain her.

Lucy wondered whether she had gone too far, but if he fired her then it would be best for both of them. There was silence from his room for the next couple of hours, and when she took in his mid-morning coffee he scarcely glanced at her.

She went for a walk at lunch time, and when she got back he had gone out. But he returned at four and began dictating, and then told her he wanted her to stay until the work was finished.

'I need both the figures and report for an early meeting tomorrow,' he told her.

It was the first time since that Saturday that he had asked her to work over, and according to Jo she was very lucky. 'It must be because you're his stepsister,' she said.

Lucy did not think so. Their unfortunate relationship made no difference to him. It was Lucy who carried all the resentment.

He left shortly after five and she carried on with the columns of figures that were beginning to make her head ache again, and the pages of detailed analytical report on some steel that was found to be inferior. Whoever was at fault would find Conan Templeton's wrath rather more than they had bargained for. He had pulled no punches in his report, and Lucy almost felt sorry for them. On the other hand, Conan had every right to be angry. His firm's reputation was at stake.

Conan, she realised, had got to the top by being tough and resilient. He stood no nonsense; he knew what he wanted and went all out to get it. His business was well organised and well run, but without his expert guidance it could easily crumble. He had high standards and made sure they were upheld. She could not help begrudgingly admiring him for it.

Lucy struggled on for another hour, and whether it was because she was thinking about Conan, or whether it was because of her headache, she found herself making the silliest mistakes which were too much to ask even her electronic typewriter to cope with. She had to retype whole pages at a time, and her waste-basket was getting fuller by the minute.

She stopped to make herself some coffee, and then wondered whether that wasn't making her head worse. She had drunk rather a lot today. She made tea instead, and when she took it back through to her office Conan was standing there.

His eyes missed nothing. The pain behind her eyes, the paleness of her cheeks, the overflowing basket. 'Have you finished?' There was an odd gentleness in his tone.

'Almost,' said Lucy.

'Then I'll wait.' And he sat down on a chair in her office.

Lucy had not realised he wanted to check through it tonight. He had said nothing about returning. She had planned to leave the report on his desk for him to go through first thing in the morning. How on earth did he think she could type while he sat there? But somehow she managed it. She took several deep, steadying breaths and then typed slowly and accurately, and in half an hour it was done.

Her mouth was dry by the time she had finished, her cup of tea cold and forgotten, her whole body aware of this man who had sat so still and silent, watching her. Once or twice she had glanced across at him, and their eyes had met and she had been startled by the intensity of his gaze. How she wished she knew what he was thinking.

She collected up the sheets of paper and handed them to him, and he took them through to his office. Lucy covered her typewriter, picked up her bag, and called out goodnight. But suddenly Conan was behind her, opening the door, seeing her through and closing it again. Together they walked along the corridor and together they went down in the lift.

'I thought you'd come back to read the report,' she said, feeling a need to fill the silence with something. Never had this lift felt so small and claustrophobic. What if it broke down? There was only the two of them in the building. They would be stuck for the whole night. She would be at his mercy. Panic tightened her throat and she broke out into a cold sweat.

He shook his head. 'I came back to check that you were all right.'

'You didn't have to.' This was idiotic. He was perfectly harmless, for goodness' sake. Just because he had kissed her a couple of times, it didn't mean he would take advantage of such a situation.

'No, I didn't, did I? But, contrary to what you might think, Lucy, I do have a caring side to my nature. Why do you think I called at your house last night?'

'I have no idea,' she answered scathingly, 'nor do I care.' She pressed her hands against the welcome coolness of the metal sides of the lift, hoping he would not notice that she had edged a few inches away from him.

His lips tightened. 'Are you afraid of me, Lucy?'

'Why should I be?' she challenged.

'There's no reason, but you look it.'

'I'm tired and——'

'Hungry?' he cut in at once. 'Not in the least looking forward to going home and cooking a meal? Nor should you. You've worked long hours today.'

And he thought she would now agree to go out to dinner with him? Lucy's eyes widened as the realisation dawned on her. So this was the reason he had asked her to work over. He hadn't really wanted that report, he had wanted to keep her here so that she would have no excuse. The nerve of the man!

'No, I'm not hungry,' she said. 'I just want to have a shower and go to bed.'

His eyes narrowed. 'Do you often skip meals?' And his gaze swept over her as though he were trying to assess whether she was losing weight.

'Only when my unthinking boss keeps me late,' she countered sharply, feeling again a blaze of sensation rip through her. Whatever else she might dislike about Conan, there was no denying his sex appeal. He wore it like a badge, and it was easy to see why each of his secretaries had been infatuated by him.

The lift reached the ground floor, and the doors opened, and Lucy felt as though she had been flung a lifeline. Even the air tasted sweeter. She did not see Conan's hurt expression as she stalked towards the main doors, but she was forced to wait for him when she discovered they were locked.

He opened them without a word and she stepped out, and while he re-locked the doors she made her way to her car. His Carrera was right next to it. The Avenger which had once been her father's looked tatty by comparison, but it was reliable, and she got in and turned the key without looking at Conan again.

But as she edged out of the car park and into the traffic, she discovered that Conan was following her. Maybe it was coincidence. Maybe he always travelled along this same stretch of road. She had no idea where he lived.

But when she turned off towards her home village and he still kept behind, chance had nothing to do with it. She was driving quite steadily, and his Porsche was capable of much higher speeds. He was definitely following her, and he must be almost stalling the high-powered vehicle.

When she got out of her car and he pulled up on the drive behind her she was livid. 'What's going on?' she demanded savagely. 'Didn't you believe me when I said I didn't want to go out with you?'

'Oh, I believed you all right.'

His smile made her suspicious. He looked like a cat who had stolen the cream. 'Then what's this all about? What are you doing here?'

'You'll see. We'll go inside, shall we?'

Much to Lucy's indignation, he produced his key and opened the door. As though he owned the place, she thought furiously. Pushing it wide, he stood back for her to enter.

Her spine was ramrod straight as she walked past him. How dared he take over like this? She heard the door close behind and she halted, turning to face him, her features contorted by the anger inside her. But before she could speak, the smell of cooking assailed her nostrils. Onions? Steak, maybe? What was going on? 'Conan?'

He saw her sniff the air and grinned. 'Dinner, my lady, will not be long. If you would care to take a shower and slip into something more comfortable...'

'Conan! What——'

He touched a finger to her lips. 'Say nothing, my lovely Lucy.'

'But——'

'We'll talk later. Run along now and make yourself beautiful for me.'

*For him!* Lucy felt bewildered, everything was getting out of hand. But the smell of food made her realise how hungry she was. So why not? But it was a one-off thing.

She would insist he never do it again. If necessary, she would have the lock changed. She didn't like the idea of his walking in here whenever he felt like it. He was beginning to take over her life.

Lucy deliberately took her time, thinking about him as she stood beneath the revitalising jets. He really did have a cheek. She was sure, when her mother had given him a key, she had not intended him to make himself so much at home.

Why had he chosen to burden himself with her? Not because he wanted to put things right, surely? Besides, nothing could alter facts. What he had done to her father was diabolical, nothing short of a crime.

Perhaps the whole affair gave him some perverse sort of pleasure? Valerie had married his father, why shouldn't he be friends with her daughter? Maybe she was a challenge? Maybe once he had won her over he would leave her alone. He had no real interest in her, nothing deep down, no fascination or attraction. It was purely a game.

But two could play games. Perhaps the quickest way to get rid of him was to let him think he was winning? To be friendly and pretend she was growing to like him.

On the other hand, it might be no game. He might have a genuine interest in her. Lord help her if he had. And to be truthful, she was no hypocrite. She could not pretend feelings she did not possess. All she could do was hope that it was not long before he got the message loud and clear.

She changed into a pretty flowered dress that swirled about her knees and had a scooped neckline and was, above all, blessedly cool. It was a warm evening, or was it because she was heated up over Conan?

When she walked into the kitchen he looked up. He wore one of her mother's plastic aprons with the words 'Master Chef' emblazoned across the front, and he looked very much at home. 'Ah, good, you're here,' he smiled. 'I was just about to come and see what was taking you so long.'

Would he really have come up to her room? wondered Lucy. Then answered her own question. Yes, he would. She would put nothing past him.

She put her head on one side and looked at him thoughtfully. 'Exactly what is it that you want from me?'

'Isn't it obvious?' he asked easily, his brows rising. 'Friendship.'

He had beautiful eyes, she thought irrelevantly. Long-lashed and dark, the whites very white, wasted on a man. 'Even though you know how I feel about you?'

'You'll change,' he said confidently.

'Oh, I will, will I?' she demanded. 'How do you make that out? You can't put the clock back.'

'No, but, given time, I can show you that I'm not as callous as you think.'

'You've already proved that you are,' she said coldly.

His lips firmed. 'One day you'll learn that in the world of business no one gets anywhere unless they're tough. But I try not to carry my ruthlessness into my private life. If you could remember that, perhaps we'll get on.'

'I don't want to get on with you,' she said bluntly, 'and I don't know why you're bothering with me.'

'You're a very attractive girl, Lucy. I want to get to know you better.'

'Despite the way I feel about you?'

'It adds to your attraction.'

'Makes me something of a challenge?'

'You could say that.' He tasted the sauce in which the steaks were cooking, and added another sprinkle of pepper.

'As I thought,' she said.

He frowned.

'All you're trying to do is make a conquest.'

Conan smiled to himself but made no comment. 'Perhaps you'd like to take your seat at the table?'

Lucy's lips were compressed as she went through into the dining-room. She was not looking forward to the meal. It was not pleasant, learning that all you were to a man was a challenge. Not that she wanted him to have any real feelings for her, but a girl had her pride.

The room overlooked the garden and the table was charmingly laid with her mother's old rose china and the crystal glasses with the green stems. Just as she was about to take her seat, the doorbell rang. When she answered it, Mike stood there. She grinned delightedly. 'Come in.' He was the very antidote she needed.

'I almost went away when I saw you had a visitor. Would you rather I did?'

'Not on your life,' answered Lucy firmly. 'I need you as I've never needed anyone before. We're just about to eat. Would you like to join us?'

And before he could answer she called out, 'Conan, we have a visitor. Will the meal stretch to three?'

Conan appeared in the kitchen doorway, apron still on, spoon in hand, a frown furrowing his brow. It changed to a glower when he saw Mike. 'Not really.'

Mike was visibly shaken by this macho man. Lucy had never described him, and the apron did nothing to detract from his powerful physique. 'It doesn't matter,' he said. 'I only came to see Lucy. I can come some other time.' And he began to back away.

But Lucy was determined. 'Nonsense, Mike. You can have some of my steak.'

Out of the corner of her eye she saw Conan's face contort with fury. She grinned and turned to him. 'Will you lay another place, or shall I?'

# CHAPTER FOUR

MIKE was clearly uncomfortable during the meal, but Lucy was having fun. She talked almost constantly to Mike about people and events that Conan knew nothing about.

'Fancy Jane marrying Guy,' she said. 'I can't believe it. They're totally unsuited. And how about Mitch? Where's he? Is he still single? He asked me to marry him, did you know that?'

Mike frowned. 'No, I never knew. I didn't realise you and he were so close.'

'Bosom friends,' she informed lightly. 'Yes, I reckon I've had more than my fair share of proposals. There was Pete, do you remember Pete?'

'Pete asked you to marry him?'

Lucy lifted her shoulders airily. 'On more than one occasion.'

'And how about you, Mike?' Conan's tone was cold. 'Are you one of the many who appear to have fallen under Miss Anderson's spell?'

Lucy gave an inward smile. *Miss Anderson!* He was angry with her. Good. Perhaps he would leave.

'I think my feelings where Lucy's concerned are private,' said Mike quietly.

Good for you too, thought Lucy. That ought to put Conan Templeton in his place.

'And so they should be,' agreed Conan, much to her surprise. 'I don't believe in telling the world how one feels, or bragging about previous conquests. It's a sign of immaturity.'

Lucy felt a surge of anger. Her face set solidly and she glared. Immature, indeed!

Conan's lips quirked as he watched her changing expression, then he pushed his chair back from the table and went out to the kitchen.

'God, I hate that man,' hissed Lucy.

'He doesn't seem a bad sort to me,' ventured Mike. 'Are you sure you're not over-reacting?'

'You know what he did.'

'Yes, but it wasn't a deliberate vendetta against your father. He just wanted what was owed to him. I can understand that.'

Lucy frowned savagely. 'You're not sticking up for Conan, for heaven's sake?'

He shook his head. 'I'm on your side, Lucy. I was just trying to put things in their right perspective.' He smiled and touched her hand across the table. 'I don't like to see you upset.'

'I'm not upset. I just wish that man had never come into my life.'

Conan returned at that moment and set the coffee-pot firmly on the table, his eyes flickering over their touching hands.

Lucy made a show of reluctantly letting Mike go, pouring their coffee, and then talking quietly to the younger man, ignoring Conan altogether. She smiled to Mike often, touching his hand or his arm, suggesting an intimacy that was non-existent.

There was a smile of cynical amusement on Conan's lips as he sat there smoking his cigar and sipping his coffee, and the more he watched them the more attentive Lucy grew towards Mike.

When they had finished their coffee she volunteered herself and Mike to wash up. 'You did all the cooking, Conan,' she said with an exaggerated smile. 'You deserve to rest.'

But he followed them out to the kitchen, leaning indolently against the door, watching them, throwing in the odd comment, making Lucy's blood boil.

The evening dragged on and on in the same vein, Lucy trying to convince Conan that there was something between her and Mike, Conan simply observing and smiling and not seeming in the least hurt that he was left out of things.

At half-past ten Mike got up to leave. She went to the door with him. 'How much longer's he likely to stay?' he muttered.

'God knows,' answered Lucy feelingly.

'I don't like leaving you with him, but he looks as though he's prepared to out-sit me. If I don't make a move, I have visions of us both being here all night.'

Lucy nodded. 'That's what I thought.'

'You think he'll go now?'

'I imagine so.'

'Why did you let him cook the meal in the first place? He's acting as though he owns the place.'

'Don't I know it,' fumed Lucy. 'He tricked me. He made me work late, and when I got back all this was arranged.'

'Are you sure you'll be all right?'

'Oh, yes, very sure. I can handle Conan, don't worry. Thanks, though, for helping me get through the evening. I do appreciate the way you played along with it.'

'Any time,' he grinned.

When she returned to the lounge Conan clapped his hands, applauding her loudly. 'Good try, but you didn't convince me.'

Lucy glared. 'I don't know what you're talking about.'

'You and Mike. Did you really think I would believe you two were attracted to each other?' His eyes widened as he asked the question. 'I'm glad I met him, actually. I can always tell when there's a spark of magic between a man and a woman, and I saw none tonight. Merely a clumsy effort for my benefit.'

'You know nothing,' she spat, furious at being found out. She had really thought she was doing a good job.

His smile was wicked. 'I know that your body responds to mine in a way it never does to your friend.'

'That's rubbish.'

'Is it?' He stood up and there was a meaningful glint in his eyes. 'Perhaps we ought to put it to the test?'

Lucy eyed him boldly. 'You touch me and I'll scream.'

'There are ways of silencing you.' His gaze flickered to her parted lips, lingering for an instant before he looked again into her eyes.

She snapped her mouth shut and tried to ignore the erratic beating of her heart. 'I'd like you to leave,' she gritted through her teeth.

'Not until I've proved something.' He looked deadly serious as he moved towards her, his eyes never leaving her face.

Lucy's chin jutted. She felt threatened. 'Get out! *Get out now!*' She wanted to rush to the front door and yank it open, but somehow her feet remained rooted to the spot.

'I asked you before, Lucy, and I'll ask you again: are you afraid of me?' He spoke softly, almost a whisper, and there was a gleam of amusement in his dark eyes.

'Not in the least.' Her chin lifted even higher.

'Good. I don't want you to be afraid of me. I like you, Lucy, I like you a lot. In fact I would go so far as to admit that my feelings go deeper than just liking you.'

Lucy frowned. 'What are you trying to say?' Surely not that he loved her? That was impossible. You couldn't love a person who never had a pleasant word to say to you, who hated you passionately, who would twist a knife in your heart rather than let you get close.

'You're an individualist, Lucy,' he said, 'although I can see a lot of your father in you. You have guts, which I admire. You have strong opinions, which you don't mind airing, and——' he added with a smile, 'when you're angry you look very sexy.'

So that was it. He saw her as a sex object. She excited him. He wanted an affair. Her eyes glittered with fury. 'I'm not flattered.'

'No?' His brows rose. 'What else would you like me to tell you?' He was inches only away from her now, and Lucy felt a prickle of heat over her skin. 'I find you very attractive, although I expect most men tell you that, and I don't like to follow the crowd. You're very feminine. I like that dress, it suits you, it softens your image. It's romantic. I thought you might have worn it especially for me?'

'Like hell I did,' she spat. 'It's cool and practical in this hot weather, that's the only reason I'm wearing it. I have no wish to please you, none whatsoever.'

'Whereas I have every wish in the world to please you, my lovely Lucy.'

Her gaze was locked to his now. She wished she knew what it was about him that did this to her. She wanted to move, to hit out at him, to run, to yell, to escape. But no, all she could do was look at him, and wait!

His hands slid behind her back, and it was as though it was all happening in slow motion. His eyes were black and consuming and sensual, and her heart raced of its own accord. One hand cradled her head while the fingers on his other hand played with her spine, feeling each vertebra in turn, starting at her nape and working right down to her lower back.

His touch was light, yet awoke her senses as though he were caressing the most intimate parts of her body. She found herself holding her breath, waiting to discover where he was going to touch her next.

She was his prisoner in mind only. She could pull away at any time, yet she was not conscious of this. It had happened before when he came near. She was bewitched. Completely captivated.

'Have you any idea what you do to me?' he asked, his voice thick and muffled as he kissed the delicate area behind her ears. 'Any idea at all?'

She knew what he was doing to her, and if his feelings were anywhere near the same, then they were in a potentially dangerous situation and she ought to get out of it now.

'I'm not conscious of doing anything,' she managed to say. 'And I wish you'd let me go. There's no point in——'

His mouth claimed hers, effectively cutting short her protest. His arms tightened, moulding her against him, and he must surely feel the erratic thump of her heart—as she felt his?

It was a timeless moment, one half of her glorying in the sensations he aroused, the other half struggling for release from this insanity. She hated him, didn't she? Why hadn't she stopped him? Why had she let herself get into this situation?

But struggling was as ineffectual as trying to escape from behind iron bars, and as his kisses became more demanding, his mouth moving expertly over hers, Lucy's efforts to free herself grew weaker and weaker until finally they were non-existent.

Her lips parted and she melted into him, accepting his kisses, glorying in them even, returning them with a degree of wantonness that later would shock her. He was taking charge of her, he was possessing her in a manner she had never dreamt of, and wave after wave of need and desire and pulsing passion racked through every nerve and every vein and every sensitive area in her body.

Tiny sounds of hunger and pleasure escaped her as his lips left her mouth to trail slowly and sensually downwards, lingering on the rapidly flickering pulse at the base of her throat. He touched it with his tongue, circling the pulse, causing it to beat even faster, and Lucy's head sank back lower and lower, and her body moved with unconscious provocation against his.

He groaned and his fingers urgently sought the neck of her dress, slipping it impatiently down over her shoulders. Lucy registered nothing except her own equally devouring need to be a part of this man.

Her dress down to her waist, the wisp of nylon and lace covering her breasts disposed of with equal haste, some of the urgency seemed to die out of him. Instead of touching her or kissing her, as she expected, he simply looked at the feminine shape of her, looked long and hard, and Lucy felt a surge of excitement, her breasts hardening beneath his inspection, her nipples erect in their rosy aureoles. Oh, God, she wanted him to touch her. Why didn't he? 'Conan?' She mouthed his name without even realising it.

'Beautiful, quite beautiful,' he said softly, almost to himself, then touched his fingers to the velvet smoothness of her flesh, trailing them over the firm shape of her, leaving not one inch undiscovered.

The very lightness of his touch did more to Lucy than if he had savaged her. Her throat contracted and felt dry, her whole body grew weak, and her eyes watched him. She caught his face between her hands and tried to urge his head down to her breasts. But he wasn't ready for that yet.

He cupped her breasts now, letting them sit in the palms of his hands. Their fullness had sometimes embarrassed Lucy, but in this moment she felt that they were beautiful too. His thumbs brushed her nipples, causing a whole new flood of sensation to rocket through her. Lucy had never known such pleasure.

She swallowed hard and ran the tip of her tongue over dry lips, and Conan looked at her, his eyes hungry, leaving her in no doubt as to the extent of his feelings.

He touched his own tongue to her lips, moistening them for her, before plundering the receptive softness within. 'You're a witch, Lucy,' he muttered.

And then at long last, at long, aching last, he moved his head to her breasts. Lucy cushioned it between her palms, her own head sunk right back on her shoulders, her expression one of exquisite torment as his lips and tongue and teeth created a whole new gamut of emotions.

He seemed to devour her, sucking her nipples, pulling, teasing, sending her half-crazy with sensations and emotions that had never surfaced before. He knew exactly what he was doing; each move, each taste, each touch, designed to arouse and excite, to make her hunger for more, to make her pliable in his hands, to make her his to do with as he liked.

Just when she thought she could stand no more of this heart-stopping torture, he lifted his head. His mouth was soft and wet, his lips darker than normal, his eyes glazed. 'God, Lucy, I must stop.' His breathing was ragged and heavy. 'Before things get out of hand.'

Her own eyes were pained, and she made an instinctive moue of disappointment.

He cupped her face between his hands and looked at her intently, a tiny smile of regret curving his lips. 'I never planned this. I never expected to—to feel as I do. I feel as though a bomb's gone off inside me. You're some woman.'

And he was some man. It was unbelievable that she could respond so completely to a man she loathed. What was the power that he held? What secret weapon? She closed her eyes and let out a shuddering sigh, and Conan echoed it. After pulling her dress back up over her breasts he gathered her to him, enfolding her in his arms. She could actually feel him trembling, could feel his heart thudding painfully, the heat of his body.

They remained locked together for a couple of long, aching minutes. Lucy felt tears on her lashes. It would come to her later that this man was still her enemy, but for the moment she needed him, needed the strength and comfort of his embrace. It had been a mind-shattering experience, one that she would re-live over and over in her memory for a long time.

He needed her too, he needed to hold her close, to hold her until the racking need that had taken hold of him had died down. They needed these minutes to come back to a normal plane.

His fingers stroked her hair and he made soothing little noises, and gradually the tension eased out of them; when he finally put her from him it was with a rueful smile.

Lucy knew she ought to rant and rave, ought to swear that if he tried any such thing again she would kill him, but for some insane reason she did not want to spoil this moment. 'I'd like you to go,' she said quietly.

To her amazement he nodded. 'I think that might be best. No regrets?'

She grimaced. 'Not at this moment, but if you hang around I can't guarantee that I won't change my mind.'

'I hope not, Lucy,' he said. 'I think we could have something good going for us.'

Lucy looked at him long and hard. 'I doubt it.'

'We'll see,' he smiled, and then turned and left without touching her again. Lucy did not even accompany him to the door, but she listened as he started the car's engine, not moving until the sound had died away.

Then she collapsed into the nearest chair. She felt ill at ease with herself, wishing she had never let him kiss her, yet still feeling the thrill of his touch, his hands on her breasts, his mouth on hers, the rasp of his tongue over her skin. It had been sheer magic. He had sent her delirious with delight, he had sent sensation after sensation riding through her body, he had given her a taste of what he would be like as a lover. He had moved the earth beneath her feet. He had rocketed her to the heavens. He had proved that he was capable of changing her mind about him.

Lucy closed her eyes, her fingers steepled together against her mouth. What was she going to do? She had just learned how easily he could get through to her. She had given so much of herself away. Too much. He had expressed a desire to repeat the exercise. He had said they had something good going for them. Had they? Could they? No, she did not think so. Conan belonged to a part of her life that was painful. He had caused the pain. She did not want an intimate relationship with him.

She heaved a sigh and pushed herself up, flicking off the light and bolting the front door before going up-stairs to the bathroom. She brushed her teeth and washed her face, shocked by the sparkle in her eyes and the warm glow to her skin.

With a groan she swung away and went to her room, pulling on her nightie and climbing into bed. She re-alised that her headache had completely gone, and she lay wide awake, looking at the ceiling, at the shaft of light slanting through a crack in the curtains from the street-lamp outside. There was only one thought in her mind. Conan Templeton.

What was she going to do about him? There was no denying the pleasure he could create. It would be a whole new life, a new existence, a new experience, but could she tolerate that from the man who had caused her father's death? Could she neatly divide the two and file them in separate compartments of her mind? The answer had to be no. There must be no repetition of what had just happened. It had been a mistake to let it happen at all.

It was a long time before she fell asleep, and it was no surprise to her that her waking thoughts were of Conan. How could she not think of him?

As usual he was at the office before her, and Lucy gave an outward show of calmness, although she was far from feeling insensitive to this man who had turned her whole world upside-down with a kiss. For her own peace of mind, though, she had to treat him with in-difference. It was the only way.

'Good morning, Lucy.' His smile was warm and wel-coming, and caused an unwanted flutter in her heart.

'Good morning,' she replied coolly, putting the letters on his desk and turning to walk out, angry with herself for responding when she had made up her mind not to.

'Lucy!'

She looked round and eyed him coldly. He was frowning.

'You can't ignore what happened last night.'

'Did something happen?' she asked, amazed to hear how steady her voice sounded.

'Don't play games,' he snapped.

Lucy lifted her fine brows. 'If anyone's playing a game, it's you. It was quite a fiasco last night, wasn't it? But I can assure you it won't happen again. I won't let it. I don't ever want you in my house. Is that understood?'

'You're making a mistake, Lucy. You're spiting yourself.'

'I know what I'm doing.'

'But do you know what you want?' He rose and came towards her, his voice a mere whisper now. 'I thought I'd persuaded you; apparently not.'

Lucy clenched her fists. If he dared touch her she would scream.

'Don't worry,' he said, 'I'm not going to force myself on you. We both know what happens when we come together. We don't need to repeat the experiment. But I don't intend giving up on you, Lucy.'

'You mean you want me to be your lover? You want an affair? Is that what you're saying?' she asked crossly. 'I won't, I tell you, *I won't*.' And with that she ran back to her own office.

What a fool she had been to let him near. What a fool to respond. Except that it had been impossible not to. He was an expert. She had succumbed willingly. She had exulted in the experience. She needed her head examining.

When Conan called her into his office later to take some shorthand, Lucy tried to pretend nothing had happened. And thankfully he, too, put their private life to one side. But it was impossible not to look at him in odd moments and recall that dark head on her breast. She could almost feel his mouth touching her.

For the first time since coming to work for Conan, Lucy was unable to read some of her shorthand, and she found it distinctly embarrassing having to ask him what he had said.

He smiled softly and repeated the sentence. But the fact that he was not irritated, the fact that he seemed to know exactly why her mind had not been on her work, made it worse, and Lucy's cheeks flamed as she left the room.

She took a stroll in the park at lunch time, and as Conan was tied up with a business meeting she did not see him again until just before she was due to go home. He came out of his office and stood in front of her desk. 'Lucy, are you free tomorrow night?'

She looked up at him sharply. 'I've told you, I want nothing more to do with you.'

'This is business.'

'In that case why didn't you say?' she snapped, feeling foolish. 'What do you want?'

'I'm having a dinner party, some important customers. I'd like you to act as hostess.'

'At your house?' she frowned.

'My apartment, yes.'

She eyed him warily.

'You don't believe me?'

'No, quite frankly I don't.'

'I'm not lying, Lucy. I'm not trying to trick you, tempting though the thought of having you in my—er— home is.'

He had been going to say bed, she felt sure. She was still not convinced. 'Who are they, these important customers?' It was odd she knew nothing about it.

'Werner Brandt and Kurt Hoeffner from Brandt, Hoeffner, GmbH, Dusseldorf. You did a letter to them the other day, remember?'

Lucy nodded. There was a chance of a big export order here. Conan had been very excited about it. Maybe he was speaking the truth, after all. 'Who normally helps you?'

'Since Norma went to America I've always entertained in hotels.'

'Norma?' frowned Lucy.

'The girl I thought I was going to marry. It didn't work out.' He sounded suddenly bitter.

'Was she your secretary?'

'Heavens, no, a childhood sweetheart.'

'What happened?'

He shrugged. 'She met someone else. That she couldn't wait while I made my millions were her exact words. She accused me of being a workaholic.'

'I see,' she said.

'No, you don't,' he replied sharply. 'But it's taught me the fickleness of women. I thought I knew Norma inside-out. She was the last person I expected to run out on me.'

Lucy wasn't surprised. Conan could not see himself as others saw him. The woman who married him would need to be a saint.

'But we're not talking about Norma,' he said firmly. 'She's water under the bridge. Tomorrow night, you have something to wear?'

'Will it be formal?'

'Of course.'

'I'm not sure that I have anything suitable,' she frowned, mentally going through her wardrobe.

'No worries,' he cut in. 'Go out tomorrow and get whatever you need. Have it charged to me.'

To her dismay Lucy realised that she had accepted the fact that she would be attending his dinner party. 'There's no need for that,' she said quietly. 'I can buy my own.'

'I insist,' he said. 'Go home now and get an early night. And by the way, you'd best pack a nightie. These dinners sometimes go on late. You may as well stay the night.'

# CHAPTER FIVE

IT WAS the dress of her dreams. Lucy had tried on several others but always came back to this one. The only thing that was stopping her was the price. She had meant it when she said she would use her own money, but this was way out of her bracket.

'It really does suit you,' encouraged the sales assistant yet again.

Lucy twirled this way and that in front of the mirror. It was midnight-blue crushed velvet, off the shoulder, mid-calf length, ruched at the sides, deceptively simple but startling. The back dipped to a low V, and its clever cut showed off her tiny waist and gently rounded hips, but somehow hid the fullness of her breasts. She liked it, she really did. The sales assistant had teamed it with a narrow velvet choker with a single diamond teardrop in the centre. Matching ear-rings were available if she wanted them.

Lucy suddenly threw caution to the winds. 'I'll take it.' And she would charge it to Conan. The diamond ear-rings, a new pair of shoes, the lot. If he wanted her to play this part, then he could jolly well pay for it. She was still annoyed by his suggestion that she stay the night. It didn't take much imagination to know why he had said that.

In order to do her shopping Lucy had left work early, and now she made her way home. Conan was sending a car to pick her up at seven, in plenty of time before his guests arrived.

She luxuriated in a long, leisurely perfumed bath and shampooed and dried her hair, then set it on large heated rollers. She made up her face carefully: shiny bronze eyeshadow, mascara to lengthen her lashes, a hint of eyeliner. Her eyes were her best feature, and she made the most of them. A touch of blusher, a dusky lipstick, and she looked like a new woman.

After taking out her rollers, Lucy carefully swept her hair up into a cluster of curls on the top of her head, teasing out tendrils to spiral against her cheeks and in her nape. She fixed the ear-rings to her ears and clipped on the choker, and finally pulled on the dramatic dress.

Her reflection was that of a stranger. Was this sophisticated woman really Lucy Anderson? Her skin had been warmed by the sun to a honey-gold tan and was silky smooth. She had used her favourite body lotion after her bath, and the delicate floral fragrance wafted in the air as she moved.

The car arrived and the company chauffeur glanced at her admiringly as she stepped out of the house. He had seen Lucy before, but never like this. She carried nothing except her silver evening bag, and felt like a queen as she slid into the limousine.

Lucy had no idea what make of car it was, but it was definitely something exotic and expensive. She sank back into the soft cream-coloured leather and let her thoughts drift to the evening ahead. She had never acted as a hostess before. On the rare occasions her father had entertained she had always gone out and left her parents to it.

Not that she foresaw any difficulties. It would simply be a matter of making sure his guests were well looked after. She wondered who was cooking the meal. Did Conan have a regular housekeeper, or was he using a firm of caterers? It was surprising how little she knew about him. And yet he knew so much about her!

The car finally stopped in front of a luxury apartment block set in spectacularly landscaped gardens. The chauffeur tapped a number into the entry-phone and Conan's voice, sounding strangely muffled through the speaker, enquired who it was. When the door was released the driver told her to take the lift to the top floor. 'Have a good evening,' he said, his face impassive, but Lucy knew what thoughts were going through his mind. If only he knew.

The lift whisked her silently and swiftly to the top, and Conan met her. He too gave a soft whistle of admiration, taking her elbow and ushering her into his elegant living-room. 'Stunning, absolutely stunning,' he said, pressing his lips to her brow. 'My guests will be knocked for six.' Then he frowned. 'Where's your bag?'

Lucy dimpled and held up the silver mesh purse.

'Your nightdress and toiletries are in there?'

'I'm not staying,' she said.

Conan frowned. 'But——'

'But nothing. I prefer my own bed, thank you very much. If your driver can't take me, I'll call a taxi.'

'You think I——'

'That's right,' she cut in sharply. 'And I don't intend repeating the other night's episode. It taught me a few things; one of them being that you're physically attractive and very persuasive. And I can't deny that it was enjoyable. But one thing it didn't do was change my mind about you.' She turned away from him and looked about the room. 'What a beautiful apartment you have.'

It was definitely a man's room, in bold browns and golds with no-nonsense furniture and very little in the way of ornaments, but as startling in its simplicity as was her dress.

She was unprepared when Conan spun her to face him. 'Don't change the subject,' he rapped. 'I have no intention of bedding you. My housekeeper has already prepared the guest-room. Is your opinion of me so low?'

'You haven't given me much reason to think otherwise,' she challenged. 'Each time we've been alone you've forced yourself on me.'

A muscle jerked in Conan's jaw. 'I have never forced myself on a woman. On both occasions you've had every opportunity to call a halt.'

Maybe she had, thought Lucy. It was confusing and totally without reason that she responded to this man she despised. Even now he was causing all sorts of unwanted emotions to spring into life inside her. He looked absolutely devastating in his white dinner-jacket.

'It occurs to me that it's yourself you're afraid of.'

'What a stupid thing to say,' she flashed.

'Is it?' he asked quietly.

'Of course. I'm my own woman. I do what I want.'

'I'd like you to be mine.'

He spoke so softly this time that Lucy only just heard. 'What a foolish fantasy,' she exploded. 'Have you really no idea how I feel? Don't you listen to what I say? Can you ever expect me to forgive you for what you did? Tonight is part of my job, you said that yourself, otherwise I wouldn't be here.' Anger gave brilliance to her eyes.

'You're fantastic!' he said.

'You're insane!'

'Am I to be spurned for the rest of my life?'

'Most definitely.'

'Your mother bears no grudges.'

Pain flickered on Lucy's face. 'She's a fool.'

'She's woman enough to realise that what happened couldn't be helped.'

'You're saying she didn't blame you for my father's death?' she asked incredulously. 'That it never even occurred to her that you were to blame?'

'Lucy, I'm not saying that at all.' His mouth firmed. 'I'm saying she had the grace to admit I couldn't have known Eric had a heart condition, and that in any case I had my own interests to consider. She said she would have done much the same in my shoes if such a vast amount of money were owed to her.'

'You had discussions with her?' frowned Lucy.

Conan nodded.

Lucy felt sickened that her mother was so weak. 'How did she meet Alan? I know you said she first met him at a meeting of the creditors, but that was a long time ago. How did they meet up again?'

'She didn't tell you?' he asked in faint surprise.

'No.'

'It seems to me that a whole lot has happened in the time you were away that your mother never told you about. Why is that, I wonder? Does she know what an acrimonious, unforgiving daughter you are?'

'She knew how I felt about your company,' retorted Lucy. 'I never made any secret of it. I thought she felt the same.'

'Perhaps falling in love with my father changed things for her.'

'It's made her soft,' she scorned.

'And you wouldn't do any such thing?'

'Never!' she claimed determinedly.

His lips quirked. 'Would you like an aperitif—some wine, perhaps?'

'Now you're changing the subject.'

A brow rose. 'Oh, no. I find it far too interesting. But you haven't answered my question.'

Lucy eyed him savagely. 'No, thanks.'

'All the same, I think you might need one.'

She frowned. 'Why?'

'I have something to tell you, Lucy. Something your mother should have told you, but clearly hasn't.'

'And the news is so bad you think I'll need a stimulant?'

He smiled faintly. 'I have a feeling you'll see it that way.'

'Try me,' she challenged, wondering what it could be.

'Very well.' He stood up and walked towards the window, looking out for a minute at the immaculate gardens before turning to face her. 'Did you ever wonder what happened to your father's business?'

'It was sold,' she informed him abruptly. 'Not that it was worth anything once you'd finished. But so long as you got what was owing you, I don't suppose you cared.'

Conan's hands clenched, but his voice was perfectly even when he spoke. 'I bought it.'

Lucy's head jerked, her eyes shot wide. '*You?* What for? What good was it to you?'

'It helped your mother, and it also helped me. With proper management it has become very profitable. Your father had some good outlets.'

She frowned ferociously. 'I bet you didn't give my mother much for it.'

'Financially it was worth nothing once all the debts were paid,' he admitted. 'But at least no one lost their job.'

'So how did it benefit my mother?'

'She became a director.'

Lucy shook her head. This was too much. 'A *director*? *My mother*?'

'And therefore earns quite a nice little income of her own.'

'I don't believe you. She would have told me. *You're lying!*'

'Am I? All you have to do is ask her.'

'Don't worry, I will,' she snapped. 'Why did she keep it a secret?'

'Isn't it obvious? What would you have said if your mother told you that she was a director of one of my companies?'

Lucy swung away in disgust. She would have called her mother every name under the sun. So this was what had been happening while she had been away. This was how her mother had met Alan. God, she felt sick. She would never have believed it possible.

'It hurts, mm?'

She closed her eyes to shut out the pain, and a few seconds later felt a glass being pushed into her hand. 'Your mother has more sense than you. You can't go through life fighting the inevitable, Lucy. Some things happen whether you want them to or not. Valerie fell in love with my father and nothing else mattered.'

Lucy sipped the brandy. 'It wouldn't happen to me.'

'Have you never been in love?' he challenged. 'Have you never felt that you wanted to spend your whole life with a man, no matter who he was or what he had done?'

Only in odd, insane moments when she had been held in a pair of arms so strong they almost crushed her, when her mouth had been captured and kissed until she had not known whether she belonged to this world or another.

But not now, not in the sane light of day when her mind was clear, not when the very man who had created these feelings was the one she hated most. 'Only fools fall in love,' she scorned.

'And Lucy's no fool, or so she tells herself.' He smiled and came to her, looking deeply into her eyes. 'Why do you fight me so? Why can't you put the past out of your mind and accept what the future has to offer?'

Lucy held his gaze for a couple of seconds, no more. 'If the future's offering me you, then I reject it wholeheartedly. I can't avoid seeing you, I realise that. Even if I gave up my job I'd still see you, but it doesn't mean I have to like you, or even be nice to you.' She shook her head. 'It's unbelievable what my mother's done. I wish she'd told me.' She took another gulp of the fiery liquid.

'I'm beginning to see why she didn't,' he said. 'You're quite a strong character, aren't you? You've always gone your own way. You've always done what you thought was right for you, and now you're wishing you could run your mother's life for her as well.'

Lifting her chin haughtily, Lucy said, 'If I'd known about Alan I'd certainly have voiced my opinion.'

'Don't you think your mother's happiness should come before anything else?'

She snorted indelicately. 'Of course I want my mother to be happy. I just can't believe that she can ignore so completely what part he played in her life.'

'Alan had nothing to do with the court case. It was my decision.'

Lucy closed her eyes, as if by shutting him out of her vision he would disappear altogether. But when she opened them he was still looking at her. He moved a step closer. 'Don't fight me, Lucy.'

'*Don't fight?*' she spat. 'My God, how can you say that when you know how I feel?' She twisted the stem of her glass round and round in her fingers.

'How do you feel?' His tone was soft and unexpectedly gentle.

He was so close that Lucy could see tiny flecks of gold in the darkness of his eyes, and every one of his thick, shadowy lashes. She could smell faintly his expensive aftershave, and was vitally aware of the rugged strength of him. Even in her anger she could not dispute that he was an attractive male animal, that it would be easy to fall under his spell and forget the part he had played in their lives.

'Well, Lucy, I'm waiting.'

'I think you already know.'

'I know your body responds to mine. I know you're fighting a monumental battle not to take what I'm offering. I know——'

'Of all the conceit!' cut in Lucy at once. 'That is not what I'm talking about.'

'So you tell me how you feel,' he said.

She looked directly into the blackness of his eyes. '*I hate you.*' Then she tossed back the rest of the brandy and slammed down the glass.

Conan glanced at her impatiently. 'I'm getting a little tired of hearing that. But isn't there some saying about hate being akin to love? That it's almost impossible to tell the difference?'

'I doubt it,' she crisped. 'They're both strong emotions, but totally opposed to one another.'

'So how do you account for the fact that although you profess to hate me—you find me physically attractive?'

'I don't know,' cried Lucy painfully. 'I wish I did. I suppose it's body chemistry, and I have no control over that, but I *do* have control over my actions.'

His smile should have warned her. It was slow and confident. She had thrown down a challenge. Before she could make a move, his arms imprisoned her and she was pulled hard against him. And the chemistry she had spoken of sprang into play.

She felt charged with sensation, pulses racing, heart thudding, blood pounding through her veins. It was insanity. She closed her eyes and tried to ignore what he was doing to her, standing as still and erect as a soldier on guard.

But when his mouth buried itself in her throat, when his hands moved possessively over her naked back, sending fresh shivers of awareness through her, Lucy found it impossible to maintain indifference. Right from the instant she had first seen him, the moment their eyes met in the church, there had been an indefinable sexual attraction. She had never been able to deny it.

Lucy made a half-hearted attempt to push him away, but when his mouth claimed hers all was lost. Her heart panicked and raced at break-neck speed, and her whole body was shocked into life. No matter what else she thought, there was no denying that physically they were perfectly compatible.

She laced her fingers through his hair, holding his head close, parting her lips beneath his persuasive mouth, drinking his kisses, feeling deliriously wanton, moving sensually against him without realising it.

His mouth sought the softness of her cheek. 'What was that you were saying about being able to control your actions?' he muttered against her ear, nibbling delicately, and then claiming her mouth again before she could respond.

Desperately Lucy tried to push herself away, but he merely chuckled and held her more tightly. The kiss lasted for ever, and when he finally let her go Lucy felt on the verge of collapse.

'I needed that, Lucy,' he said quietly. 'I think you did, too. I think the evening will be an unqualified success.'

Lucy glared. 'I doubt it. Heaven knows why I let you kiss me.'

'Because you're seeing sense at last. Because you're beginning to realise it's no use fighting the inevitable.'

Her fine brows rose. 'You thought it inevitable that I would succumb?'

He chuckled. 'As inevitable as spring follows winter. Shall I show you round before my guests arrive?'

Lucy did not answer, merely following him automatically. She was insane, she was a weak-minded fool. How could she let him kiss her? Why hadn't she stopped him? What sort of an evening was it going to be now?

'The dining-room,' he announced unnecessarily.

A beautiful room with an oval rosewood table and matching chairs, the seats upholstered in rose-coloured velvet, a dark green carpet covering the floor. The table was beautifully laid with crisp damask napkins folded in the shape of fans, gleaming silver and sparkling crystal. Two green candles sat in delicate green holders at either end of the table, and in the centre was a charmingly unusual arrangement of wild roses.

'Mirry's handiwork, not mine.' And at her frown. 'My housekeeper.' Come, I'll introduce you. She's a treasure.'

The housekeeper had her back to them in the spotless kitchen, but as they entered she swung round. Lucy stifled a gasp. The girl was beautiful. It wasn't some middle-aged woman, as she had expected, but a shapely brunette in her late twenties. What sort of a treasure did Conan mean? And why couldn't he have asked this girl to help him host his dinner party? She would have been a wow with his guests. And most definitely she was in love with Conan. It was there in her eyes. They were wide and beautiful and intent upon his face.

'Lucy, meet Miranda. Mirry, this is Lucy Anderson. I told you about her, remember?'

His way of speaking had changed, he was enunciating his words more clearly. Lucy had been watching the other girl, feeling an odd sort of pain that they shared this house together. Now she turned to look at Conan with a faint frown.

'Mirry's deaf and dumb,' he explained softly.

Lucy felt instant compassion. Her own problems were as nothing compared to the cross this girl had to bear. 'Hello, Mirry,' she said, holding out her hand.

Miranda's response was like the sun coming out from behind the clouds. Her smile lightened her whole face and she took Lucy's hand firmly in hers. Then her hands and fingers moved in swift sign language that meant nothing at all to Lucy.

But Conan was watching his housekeeper. 'She says Lucy's a lovely name, and you're lovely too. She hopes we enjoy her cooking and that the evening will be a success.'

Lucy looked at him incredulously. 'You understand her?'

He nodded.

'Can you do sign language as well?'

In answer he demonstrated his skill, and there followed a rapid silent conversation between him and Mirry which ended with him chuckling in delight.

'What were you saying?' Lucy felt sure the joke was at her expense, yet she smiled too. He amazed her, he really did. Who would have thought that a man as ruthless and as callous as Conan would employ a deaf and dumb housekeeper and take the time to learn sign language so that they could communicate? Obviously there was a side to him that she had yet to see. Conan the compassionate did not add up with the image she had formed in her mind.

'She said she thinks you will make me an excellent wife and that we should make beautiful children together.'

'No?' Lucy looked at him in shocked disbelief. 'I hope you put her right?'

'Most definitely I did. Mirry understands perfectly now what sort of a relationship you and I have.'

'Like the fact that I despise you? That tonight is part of my job and nothing else?'

'But of course.'

His answer was too smooth. Lucy eyed him sceptically.

Mirry was watching them both and an anxious frown creased her brow. She signed something quickly to Conan.

He smiled instantly, and whatever his response it seemed to reassure the other girl. She touched Conan's shoulder and kissed his cheek, and Lucy wondered at such intimacy between employer and employee. Not that it bothered her, of course, she told herself firmly. Conan's private life was his own affair.

'We'll let Mirry get on,' he said, and once they were outside the kitchen he added, 'She's quite a girl.'

Lucy nodded. 'Was she born like that?'

'Yes. It's very sad. Her parents were friends of my parents. Patricia was over forty when Mirry was born.

She was their only child. They had waited so many years, and then this. They tried to teach her at home but eventually had to send her to a special school. One day, on their way to visit her, they had an accident. They both died.'

'How awful,' said Lucy, her face pained at the very thought of it.

'She had no other family, so when she left school she came to us. She went to college and is now a qualified cook, but no one wants to employ her.' There was a sudden fierce bitterness to his tone. 'Hence her coming to work for me.'

It was a sad story. Lucy sympathised deeply with the girl. 'Does she sleep here?'

He glanced at her with a smile lifting the corners of his mouth. 'What do you think?'

'Knowing you, I imagine she does.'

'And that bothers you, does it?'

'Did I say that?' she asked loftily.

'No, but it was there all the same. Actually she shares a flat with another girl. It wouldn't be right and proper to sleep here, she said, even though I did suggest it.'

I bet you did, thought, Lucy. Despite her handicap, Miranda was a girl no man would be able to resist. There had to be something going on between them, and surprisingly the thought hurt.

'Here's the room I had prepared for you.' They had moved away from the kitchen and along the corridor, and now he pushed open another door. The room echoed the pink and green theme of the dining-room and there was even a bowl of wild roses on the dressing-table. It smelled of polish and freshly laundered linen and was very inviting.

'I'm sorry if I've put Mirry to unnecessary trouble,' said Lucy quietly.

'Who knows,' he smiled, 'you might use it yet. The night is young. Good food, good wine and good company can change many a person's mind.'

Lucy said nothing, but she knew that he would never persuade her to stay.

'The bathroom is through here.' It was a dream in palest aqua with gold-plated accessories and deep sea-green rugs and towels. There was a shower as well as a bath, and it was almost as big as the bedroom.

'Tempted yet?'

She shook her head.

He shrugged. 'The master bedroom next.'

As he flung the door wide Lucy was shocked by a bold black and white colour scheme with splashes of vivid red in the form of cushions and lampshades. There was lots of chrome and glass and white fur. It was distinctive but definitely not relaxing, and she knew that if she were married to Conan she would want to alter it. She could never sleep there. Immediately she was horrified that such a thought had entered her mind.

'Do you like it?'

'It's—different,' she admitted.

'I inherited it, actually, but it's grown on me. It's a very practical room.' He glanced at the black and white clock on one wall. 'I think we should prepare ourselves for our guests. They'll be here any minute.'

*Our* guests! Lucy did not correct him, but there was no way she wanted to be linked with Conan, and her back was stiff with resentment as they returned to his comfortable lounge.

Within seconds his visitors arrived and introductions were made. Kurt Hoeffner was blond and stocky, with piercing blue eyes and gold-rimmed glasses. He was no older than Conan, and he looked at Lucy with open appreciation. Werner Brandt, on the other hand, was nearing sixty, with snowy white hair and a moustache. He was lean and tall and held himself erect. 'This is your wife?' he asked Conan as he shook Lucy's hand.

Conan smiled. 'Unfortunately, no.'

Lucy shot him a quick glance. He sounded regretful, or was it all show?

'She's my secretary—but also my stepsister and—very good friend.'

'One day, maybe?' asked Werner Brandt with a twinkle in his eyes.

Lucy contained her anger with difficulty, fixing a smile to her lips. 'Who knows?'

The evening on the whole was quite successful. She sat opposite Conan, with the two Germans on either side of her, and the conversation centred inevitably on the steel industry. Lucy had learned a little bit during the short time she had been working for Conan, and was able to throw in the odd comment which seemed to earn his approval.

Miranda served the main courses, then quietly left the house, and it was up to Lucy to dispense the coffee in the lounge.

She had drunk copious quantities of wine, her glass being topped up by Conan each time she emptied it. And now he was offering her brandy.

'No, thank you,' she said softly.

'Lucy, you must.' This was Kurt Hoeffner. 'Come, we will sip together and get quietly drunk while these two carry on with their business. They will not even notice.'

It was true that Werner and Conan had done most of the talking, but on the other hand Conan had not ignored Lucy. His eyes had been on her often, and they had sent swift and unwanted warmth speeding through her limbs.

Without giving her time to protest, Kurt picked up her coffee and brandy, setting them down beside his own on a low table in front of the settee. Once, during the course of the evening, Lucy had felt his ankle against hers. She had thought that maybe he had touched her accidentally while stretching out his legs, but now she realised that it had been intentional.

He sat close, too close, and his tone was soft and intimate. 'You are beautiful. *Schöne*. Conan is a fool if he does not marry you quickly.'

'We don't have that sort of relationship,' she said primly, trying to edge away, but his hand on her leg stopped her.

Lucy saw Conan watching them out of the corner of his eye and perversely put her hand on top of Kurt's, looking into his eyes as though she were hanging on to his every word.

'Lucy, Werner would like more coffee.'

The sharp command rang across the room, startling Lucy and telling Kurt in no uncertain terms that Conan did not approve of his behaviour.

Kurt shrugged and smiled ruefully. 'You can't blame me for trying.'

Lucy grinned too, glad this man was not angry. She privately thought that Conan had been too abrupt.

'I think,' said Kurt Hoeffner in a careful whisper, 'that he is jealous.'

Conan, jealous? What a laugh! He didn't feel that way about her at all. But when the two men had gone and Lucy was about to ask whether she could ring for a taxi he rounded on her furiously. 'What was that all about?'

'What?' she asked innocently, the incident already forgotten.

'You and Kurt.'

She smiled cynically. 'He said you were jealous.'

'And he's damn well right. Insanely jealous. Haven't you guessed how I feel about you?'

'What do you mean, how you feel?'

'I love you, Lucy.' He made no attempt to touch her. He simply stood and waited for his profound statement to take effect.

# CHAPTER SIX

LUCY refused to believe that Conan loved her. He desired her, yes. He coveted her body. But that was all. To declare that he loved her was ridiculous.

'You don't believe me?' He took in her astonished expression, his own fierce anger fading, to be replaced by a faint frown.

'It wouldn't matter if I did,' she returned. 'I don't love you.'

'You're still determined to hold the past against me?'

She eyed him steadily, resolutely fighting the power he seemed to hold over her. 'It would be sacrilege to my father's memory if I forgave you.'

'You're fighting your own instincts, you do realise that?' There was sudden impatience in his voice.

Lucy shrugged. 'I can't help how I feel.'

'Too true you can't help it. Your body responds to mine as if you were my own other half. Explain that away if you can.'

'Easily,' she snapped. 'What I feel for you is nothing more than physical.' She paused and met his eyes coolly. 'Whatever happens between us, be very sure of one thing, I will never fall in love with you. You're wasting both your breath and your time if you think that.'

Conan closed the gap until they were separated by no more than an inch, and she could feel the very strong and very real magnetism that pulled them together. His eyes did not waver from hers, and in their depths was a mixture of pain and desire. 'Lucy, you don't know what you're saying. You're not giving yourself time.'

'I know exactly what I'm saying.' Lucy found it difficult to hold his gaze at such close proximity. But whatever hostility she might feel, however much she loathed him, there was no denying the strength of his physical attraction. It angered her that she responded so readily, and this anger was reflected in her next words. 'For goodness' sake, Conan, doesn't plain speaking make any difference? Just get away from me and keep away. I think it would be best if I gave up my job. It's not going to work out. I thought it might, but——'

'Lucy.' He gripped her arms suddenly and strongly, his eyes intent on hers. 'It would if you'd let it. Try to push out of your mind who I am or what you think I am. Take me at face-value.'

'I can't,' she whispered, agonised. 'I can't. Memories are too vivid.'

'Only because you insist on keeping them alive.'

'How can I help it when I see you every day?'

'Your mother managed to forget, and surely Eric's death affected her far more deeply?'

'I suppose so,' said Lucy slowly, and yet her mother, even in those early days, had never blamed C.T. Steels. It was Lucy who had done all the ranting and raving and accusing. Lucy had been the one who swore never to forgive the man responsible. For two years these thoughts and feelings had been firmly implanted in her mind, and it was not easy to dismiss them now.

'How about calling a truce, Lucy? I won't push you, no strings attached, nothing. Just friendship, if that's all you want, but not this burning hatred that's doing neither of us any good.'

Lucy felt tempted. Something was happening, despite the harsh unforgivingness inside her. She was already tired of the conflict. She was attracted to Conan whether she liked it or not. 'No more declarations of love?' she asked warily.

'None.'

'Just—friendship?'

He nodded.

'It's all you'll ever get, Conan,' she warned him. 'I can't go any further, I'm sorry. And I'd like to go home now. Will you call me a taxi?' Her tone was quiet and subdued, and Conan must have realised what an effort it had been for her to make this concession.

He spoke gently. 'I'll take you myself.'

'No, Conan,' she said at once. 'I need to be alone.' And reluctantly he let her go.

Lucy slept little that night. Conan's declaration of love had stunned her, and she was still not sure whether she believed him. How could he love her and accept only friendship in return? If the positions were reversed, Lucy knew she would never be able to do that.

When she awoke the next morning Lucy felt strangely excited. Conan was right when he said it was wrong to bear a grudge for so long. She would do her very best to forget who and what he was, and enjoy a healthy friendship.

In the days that followed Lucy realised a new kind of happiness. Conan, true to his word, never forced the pace. There were times when she longed for his kisses, when she hungered to feel his arms about her, but he seemed content with the way things were, and Lucy had no intention of making the first move.

They were a team at the office and they were friends out of it. Sometimes he took her out for a meal; occasionally she asked him back home and cooked dinner for them. But he never took her to his apartment again, and there were nights when they did not even see each other. Lucy was surprised how much she missed him on these occasions. Mike came round once or twice, but when he discovered that she was dating Conan his visits became less frequent until she hardly saw him at all. 'I always knew you were protesting too strongly,' he said. 'If he's the man you want, I hope you'll be very happy.'

'It's nothing like that,' she informed him firmly. 'We're friends, that's all.'

But Mike hadn't believed her, and Lucy was discovering that she wanted more from Conan than just friendship. It irked her that he no longer tried to kiss her. She knew he wanted her, because she had seen the look in his eyes in unguarded moments, and she wondered how he managed to control his actions.

But his control finally snapped when they collided in his office doorway one night when they were both working late. He instinctively put his arms around her, and the next second she was pulled hard against him. 'Lucy,' he groaned. 'Oh, God, Lucy.'

It was the first time he had held her since she had made her pact, and the effect was devastating. It set off a chain reaction in every pulse and nerve until her whole body throbbed.

'Have you any idea what you've been doing to me?' His face was creased in anguish, he looked in actual physical pain. 'How much longer have I got to wait before I dare touch you? Before I kiss you? Before I——'

Lucy silenced him by lifting her face and touching her lips to his. She was ready for him now.

With a further groan his arms tightened and they kissed with animal hunger, and all the pent-up emotions that had been building over the days bubbled up inside them and welled over. They clung to each other as if they never wanted to let go, and it seemed a lifetime before he finally dragged his mouth away from hers.

'Lucy?' he asked wonderingly, his eyes dark and still full of unreleased passion, 'does this mean that you're finally beginning to care for me? Dare I hope that——'

'Don't push me,' she murmured. She felt deliriously, wonderfully alive, but she was not ready for a commitment, not yet. There was still a long way to go.

But as more days slid by their relationship underwent a subtle change. She thought less and less about Conan as a friend and more and more about him as a lover.

He kissed her often now, and she grew increasingly responsive. Sometimes she wondered how he managed to call a halt. They were halcyon days, and she was very, very happy.

Another card came from the newlyweds. The message was brief. 'What an experience. We are seeing some spectacular sights.'

It was unlike her mother to write so little, thought Lucy. Usually her holiday cards were packed with information. She smiled to herself. Obviously her mother had other things on her mind.

Then one evening, when she had invited Conan back for a meal, the doorbell rang and confronting Lucy was a lean, grey-haired man with a gaunt face and a worried expression. His skin was pale beneath his tan and he did not look at all well. She almost did not recognise him.

'Lucy, is your mother in?'

'It's Martin Goodfellow, isn't it?' She frowned, her heart suddenly lurching.

He nodded.

Everything came rushing back with a vengeance. 'You have a nerve, coming here,' she accused him. 'I can't believe it! Don't you know what you've done?' Her voice rose shrilly, total anger consuming her that the man who had swindled her father out of so much money should calmly turn up on their doorstep. 'My father's dead because of you. Go away. *Go away!*'

The man's shoulders sagged and he looked on the verge of collapse. 'Lucy, I know how you must feel, but believe me, if I could change things I would.'

'Why have you come back?' she demanded sharply.

His thin lips twisted and he looked as though he needed to sit down, but Lucy had no intention of asking him in. 'For several reasons,' he said, 'but one of them was because my conscience was troubling me. Never let love blind you to all that is sane and sensible, Lucy. It's what I did, and it was the biggest mistake of my life.'

'Really?' she demanded coldly.

'When I found out that my best friend had died—taking the blame for what I had done—I was utterly devastated. It's taken me days to pluck up the courage to come here. But I must see Valerie. I must make my peace with her.'

'Who is this, Lucy?' A hand on her shoulder made her whirl. She met Conan's curious dark eyes.

'Martin Goodfellow,' she answered abruptly.

Conan looked surprised and he frowned as he saw the tight anger on her face. 'What does he want?'

'To see my mother.'

'I'll have a word with him,' he said softly. 'You go back into the kitchen.' He touched her cheek and smiled, and Lucy allowed herself to smile weakly in return.

But her smile turned to anger when the minutes ticked away and there was no sign of Goodfellow leaving. Conan had taken him through to the lounge, and the soft murmur of their voices went on and on.

In the end she could stand it no longer. She pushed open the door, her green eyes flashing. If Conan could not get rid of him, then she would do it herself.

She could not believe the picture that met her eyes. They stood near the window, each enjoying a glass of her mother's whisky, looking for all the world like old friends. Martin Goodfellow's face had regained some of its colour, and he was laughing over something Conan had said.

'What's going on?' she demanded harshly.

They turned at the sound of her voice. Conan smiled and took a step towards her, while the older man looked suddenly uneasy again.

'Lucy,' said Conan persuasively, 'Martin's been telling me his story. He's truly repentant for what he did. His life's been hell this last couple of years.'

Her chin was high. 'Really? I can just imagine what it was like living in the lap of luxury on my father's money. Some hell.' She looked hostilely at Martin Goodfellow and he averted his gaze.

'Lucy, it's taken Martin a lot of courage to come here today.'

'He shouldn't have bothered,' she snapped. 'I'm not interested in anything he has to say. But I might have known you'd take his side. You have a lot in common. The two of you between you killed my father.'

'I think I'd better go,' said Martin Goodfellow, shuffling across the room.

Lucy stood back to let him pass, all the hatred that had built up over the last two years boiling inside her. When he had left the house she rounded on Conan. 'I think you'd better go as well.' God, how she hated him in this moment. If he hadn't taken the other man's side it might not have been so bad, but to see them drinking and laughing like two old buddies was more than she could stand.

But Conan made no attempt to move. 'You were pretty hard on him.'

'With every right,' she spat. 'I thought you were going to get rid of him for me. What happened? Did you believe his sob-story?'

'He's had a pretty hard time of it.'

'Am I supposed to feel sympathy?' she charged. 'Are you forgetting my father's dead because of him—and *you*.' He flinched visibly, but she was past caring and went on, 'You stood there talking to him, plying him with my mother's whisky, and yet you expect me to say nothing. God, you don't know me.' Her throat contracted painfully and she fought back sobs of frustrated anger. 'Just go away.'

But Conan stood his ground, his jaw clenched, his eyes cold. 'Are you going to carry this resentment to your grave? Have you any idea what it's doing to you? What it's turning you into? Lord, I thought you were beginning to come to your senses. I thought I was getting somewhere. It looks as though I'm back to square one.'

'Perhaps it's just as well.' She eyed him aggressively. 'It will always be there. I shall never be able to forget.'

'We all make mistakes, Lucy.'

'At the cost of someone else's life?' Her tone was barely civil.

'Do you think Martin doesn't regret what he did? It's cost him more than it cost you.'

Lucy's head jerked. 'How can you say that?' She had lost her father, for heaven's sake. Had he no idea at all what that had done to her?

'Martin lost everything,' he said quietly. 'First, his lady-love left him when the money ran out. Apparently she had very expensive tastes—the reason he embezzled your father's funds. He was besotted with her.'

'I have no sympathy,' she said coldly.

'Then his wife died. Arriving home for the funeral, he discovered that his best friend was dead also. He had no idea anything had happened to your father. The guilt is almost more than he can stand. He has no family. They never had any children. His wife was a paraplegic. She had an accident shortly after they were married and never walked again. He's a broken man, Lucy. How can you go on hating him?'

Lucy swung away. Put like that, how could she? There seemed no end to Martin's suffering, and she wasn't totally insensitive. But it wasn't easy to forgive, either. She had just discovered it was easier to remember her hatred.

'I'll go now, Lucy,' he said. 'I think I've left you with enough to think about.'

She did not even turn round. Conan at this moment was a cold stranger, and she wanted nothing more to do with him.

Lucy could not get Martin Goodfellow's tragic story out of her mind. He had come to beg forgiveness and she had reacted with violence. What must he be thinking?

It was a pity he had chosen a time when her mother was absent, because Valerie would have reacted very differently. She had a much larger capacity for forgiving.

And it was futile now to hope that she and Conan could ever make a go of things. Hadn't she just proved how easily she could flare up and lash out at him? It simply wouldn't work. It wasn't fair on Conan.

Lucy almost did not go to work the next day. But that was the coward's way out, she told herself, and whatever else she might be she was not a coward. It came as an anticlimax, therefore, to find a note on her desk and no Conan.

> Lucy, I have to go away for a few days. A sudden urgent call from Germany. It is perhaps for the best. It will give you the time that you seem to need to come to terms with yourself.

There followed a few instructions regarding work, and it was signed, 'Yours, Conan.'

Lucy's lips were compressed as she tore the note into shreds and threw it in the bin. 'Yours, Conan.' No love, nothing. Had it died for him already? It had been a short, bitter-sweet relationship, but it could never have worked.

Conan returned to the office four days later. It was almost five and Lucy was about to go home. 'Lucy,' he acknowledged as he closed the door behind him.

'Hello, Conan,' she said softly, and cursed her heart for fluttering insanely. This wasn't what she had planned at all. His black hair had been recently cut, and when she looked at him Lucy felt her resolve fading.

'Are you not well, Lucy?'

She swallowed hard. 'I am perfectly well, thank you.'

'You look pale and tired.'

'I've not been sleeping too well,' she admitted.

'You've been thinking about us? Have you reached a decision?'

Lucy had not expected him to put the question so quickly, but she was glad that he had. 'Yes, Conan, I've decided that no good can come of a continued relationship. I think it would be best if we didn't see each other again. I'd like to leave straight away.'

Lucy saw the sharp stab of shock in his eyes before he guarded them. 'And all this has been brought about by Martin Goodfellow's untimely visit?'

'I think it was a good thing that he came,' she answered bluntly. 'You saw how I reacted, and if I'm to be totally honest, anything could trigger me off. I can't forget what you did, Conan, no matter how I try.'

'I think you're over-reacting.' He eased his fingers around the neck of his collar as though it was strangling him, even though his two top buttons were undone.

'I don't think so,' said Lucy.

He pushed himself up and stood with his back to her, looking out of the window, but she could see his reflection and the grim lines round his mouth. And she wanted to go to him and hold him. It hurt so much. Why couldn't she forgive him? Why couldn't she forget? Why was it so hard?

'The decision is yours, Lucy.' His voice sounded dead.

She closed her eyes, and when she opened them he had turned and was looking at her. He held out his hands and after only a moment's hesitation she took them and let him pull her to her feet. 'I can't believe this is happening,' he said grimly.

Lucy's heart was pounding fit to burst, and his touch sent all sorts of unwanted sensations through her veins. Her eyes locked into his and it was as though he was willing her to change her mind. For several long seconds they looked at each other, and as though drawn by a magnet their heads moved slowly forward.

He was going to kiss her, Lucy knew that, and there was nothing at all she could do to stop him. She wanted it as much as he did. Her lips parted, and when his mouth finally claimed hers she heard bells ringing in her head.

Then came Conan's growl of annoyance. 'Dammit!' he snarled, and Lucy realised that it was the telephone.

He snatched up the receiver and barked into it, and then his tone changed, became suddenly concerned. 'Of course I'll come and pick you up. What time? Right, I'll be there.'

Lucy frowned as she met his eyes. 'Who was that?'

'My father. They're coming home.'

Panic raced through her. 'What's happened?'

He touched her shoulder. 'Your mother's been plagued by seasickness, a bad case of it every time they leave port. Apparently she can't stand it any longer, so Alan's bringing her home.'

'Poor Mom,' said Lucy, sorry for her parent, but relieved it was nothing worse. 'It's the first time she's been on a ship, and she was so looking forward to the cruise. I'll come with you.'

'No,' crisped Conan at once. 'You go home and make sure everything's ready.'

'But you'll be away hours.'

'I'm going alone.' His tone brooked no argument.

Lucy guessed he would have taken her if things had been different, if she hadn't ruined their budding relationship. Now he couldn't stand the thought of several hours in her company.

But it was her mother who was ill, after all. She had every right to go with him. She tried again. 'I want to come, Conan. You're being totally unfair. She might need me.'

He looked at her impatiently. 'Your mother has Alan.'

And there it was in a nutshell. Alan was now the mainstay in her mother's life. Alan had replaced Eric. It hit her forcefully that Conan, as a member of the family, was also a permanent part of her life, whether she liked it or not. There would be no avoiding him unless she left home altogether.

She could see years and years of pain stretching ahead of her, needing him physically and yet hating him, never ceasing to feel resentment for the part he had played in their lives.

He left the office, and the kiss that the phone had interrupted was never finished, and there probably wouldn't be another opportunity. Lucy unconsciously lifted her chin. It was just as well. When Conan kissed her she became a different person; she forgot everything that he stood for and let her heart rule her head.

It was the early hours of the morning when she finally heard his car pull up on the drive. She had polished her mother's bedroom and put fresh sheets on the bed and a small vase of marguerites on the dressing-table. She had made sure everywhere was clean and welcoming, and was dozing in an armchair when they arrived.

Her mother looked drawn and pale, in contrast to Alan's healthy tan, and Lucy hugged her anxiously. 'Would you like some tea or coffee, or perhaps a brandy?'

Valerie shook her head. 'What I'd really like is to go to bed.'

'It's all ready,' said Lucy. 'Come on, I'll take you up.'

'No need,' said Alan at once. 'I'm in need of some shut-eye myself. We'll go together.'

'I'll see you in the morning, love,' smiled her mother. 'I'm sure I'll feel much better after a night's sleep in my own bed.'

It was odd watching the two of them go upstairs, Alan about to take the place of her father in her mother's bed. Lucy experienced a peculiar pang of pain. He would never take her father's place, not in her mind.

She turned, and Conan was eyeing her. 'You'll have to get used to it,' he said softly. 'Would you feel like this about any man your mother married, or is it because it's Alan?'

'I think you know,' she snapped.

His eyes hardened. 'I think it's time I turned in, too.' And at the sudden raising of her brows. 'As it's late, your mother suggested I use the spare room. I trust you have no objections?'

'Would it matter if I had?'

He gave a mirthless smile. 'Not in the least. Good-night, Lucy. Pleasant dreams.' And he too went upstairs.

Lucy stood and fumed for a minute before turning out the lights and following. She met him on the landing as he came out of the bathroom. He touched a finger to her cheek. 'Did I ever tell you, Lucy, that I sleep-walk?'

Her eyes shot wide. 'You dare come into my room and I'll—— '

'Scream?' he suggested, a mocking gleam in his eyes. 'And wake your mother, when she's not feeling too good? Shame on you. I'm sure that if we tried we could be as quiet as two church mice.'

He grinned at her outraged expression. 'Don't get carried away, you're quite safe. I prefer my women willing. Goodnight again.'

Lucy heard him moving about in the room next to hers and she had a sudden swift vision of his hard, tanned body divested of all its clothes. Shivers of desire ran through her limbs, and she knew that if he came to her room she would be unable to fend him off.

She wanted him, oh, so much. For a few days he had made her happier than she had ever been in her life. Just thinking about the time they had spent together made her heartbeats quicken. She heard the creak of the bed— and then all was silent.

What was he thinking? she wondered. About her? Was he wishing that things had turned out differently? Or was he already slipping into the realms of sleep? He had had a long drive, after a day already spent travelling. He must be exhausted. She slid into bed herself, and in no time at all was asleep.

When she awoke it was almost nine. Lucy looked in horror at the clock. In the excitement of her mother coming home she must have forgotten to set the alarm. Still bleary-eyed, she went downstairs to make a much-needed cup of tea. To her dismay Conan sat in the kitchen and, annoyingly, he looked as though he had had a full night's sleep instead of a scant five hours. His eyes were bright, his hair neatly combed, even his trousers and shirt still looked neatly pressed.

He motioned her to sit down. 'Something tells me you won't be going to the office today?'

She eyed him suspiciously. 'I don't have the kind of boss who'd allow that.'

'Oh, I don't know,' he said. 'He can be very reasonable. Perhaps you've never given him a chance? If I were you, Lucy, I'd go and wake myself with a shower, by which time I'll have breakfast ready.'

Lucy needed no second bidding. She quickly washed and dressed in a cotton skirt and blouse, and when she went back downstairs she found Conan in the dining-room, a check cloth on the table, her mother's yellow breakfast-set looking cheerful on this rather grey morning. The sun had completely disappeared, and sultry clouds hung in the sky.

He placed a boiled egg before her, and the toast was crisp and golden. There was fresh orange juice as well as tea and a pot of marmalade. Lucy was impressed. He would make some woman a good husband. What a pity it wouldn't be her.

'Have you had second thoughts about your decision?'

His question surprised her. She had been staring out at the garden watching a cat stalking a bird, his body flattened to the ground, each step slow and calculated, and she had not realised that Conan was studying her.

'What decision?' she frowned, turning her attention reluctantly to him.

'That you don't want to see me again. That you want to throw in your job.'

She looked down at her egg, slicing off the top and sprinkling it with salt before answering. 'I think it's best.'

'Why?'

Her tone grew impatient. 'I've explained to you why.'

'I don't accept it.'

She paused in the act of putting a spoonful of egg into her mouth. 'I'm afraid you'll have to.'

'Lucy.' He waited until she had emptied her spoon, then he put his hand on her wrist to prevent her from taking another mouthful. 'You're making a big mistake.'

'I'm not.' She shook her head forcefully. 'I've given it a lot of thought, Conan.'

'So have I. And I've decided that I can take whatever you dish out. I think the love you feel for me—a love not yet admitted, but there all the same—easily outweighs any other reservations you might have.'

Lucy looked at him. 'You sound very confident.'

'I am. I love you too, Lucy, and I intend to marry you. I'm not going to let you walk out on me.'

*Marriage!* He was talking about marriage? 'Conan, you've really no idea how I feel, have you? I don't love you, can't you understand that? I resent you, I can't help it. It would be wrong to marry you. I couldn't make you happy. There's far too big a barrier between us.'

He took the spoon out of her fingers and held both her hands in his. 'But it's not insurmountable.'

She closed her eyes, feeling the torture of having him touch her. Her whole body sprang to life, responding to him with a wantonness that had become achingly familiar. How could she live without this man? What was she doing to herself?

'Lucy, look at me.'

She obeyed his soft command and there was pain on his face too. Naked pain, and hunger and need and desire. 'Don't do this to me, Lucy.'

A shudder racked through her, and the next moment they were locked in an embrace that shut out the rest of the world. His mouth found hers and they drank from each other, and gave themselves, and when Alan Templeton entered the room neither of them heard.

# CHAPTER SEVEN

'GOOD morning, Mother, how are you feeling?' Lucy stood beside her mother's bed with a tray of tea in her hand, her cheeks still burning from the embarrassment of Alan finding her and Conan in an embrace.

Valerie was propped up against the pillows, looking a whole lot better, and she smiled in surprise when she saw her daughter.

'Lucy, how lovely. Why aren't you at work?'

Lucy set her mother's tea down on the bedside table. 'I overslept and so Conan's given me the day off.'

'You're enjoying your work?'

Lucy nodded. 'Very much so.'

'I'm pleased. I'm glad you've settled down. Your father and I were very worried when you first left school. I've thought about you often while we were away.' She picked up her cup and took a sip. 'How are you getting on with Conan?'

'All right, I suppose,' she said quietly.

But there must have been an inflection in her voice that made her mother look at her sharply. 'Is there something I should know?'

Lucy sat down on the edge of the bed and began twisting the sheet between her fingers. 'I've seen quite a lot of him, actually, and—I think he's in love with me.'

'That's wonderful.' Valerie's face lit up with happiness. 'How do you feel about him?'

'I don't think that matters,' said Lucy, adding accusingly, 'Why didn't you tell me who Alan was?'

'Lucy, what's done is done,' replied her mother calmly. 'There's no point in bearing malice. Do you love Conan?'

'He killed Daddy,' she choked, ignoring her mother's question.

'Your father's heart gave up on him, that's what happened,' corrected Valerie. 'It was nothing to do with Alan, or Conan, or anyone else. Eric was a sick man. He had been for years. He should have been taking it easy but he wouldn't. I knew, and he knew, that one day it would happen.'

'But if there hadn't been that court case——'

'It would have been something else, Lucy.' She looked at her daughter keenly. 'You're not holding it against Conan?'

Her reply was no more than a whisper. 'I can't help it.'

'Oh, Lucy, love, come here.' Her mother pulled her into her arms and for a few seconds tears rolled down both their faces, then Valerie held her daughter from her and said, 'If I have no hard feelings, Lucy, then you shouldn't. I lost my best friend, my lover and my husband. You lost your father. I love Alan, but he will never replace Eric. They are two totally different men whom I love in different ways. But I'm very happy. For a time I never thought I would be again. And I don't want you to ruin your chance of happiness through misguided loyalty.'

Lucy clung to her mother for a moment longer. 'Why didn't you tell me Conan had bought Dad's business— and that he had made you a director?'

'Because you wouldn't have liked it. I intended telling you, but in my own good time, when I thought you were ready for it.'

'It was a shock, learning it from Conan.'

Her mother nodded. 'I expect it was.'

They were silent for a moment and then Lucy said quietly, 'Martin Goodfellow's back.'

She felt a tiny tremor run through the slender frame of her parent, but Valerie's voice was perfectly steady when she spoke. 'You've seen him?'

'He came here, looking for you. He didn't know about—Daddy. It upset him, I think. His wife's died as well, and his mistress has left him. He—he's—pretty broken up.' But he was alive. *Alive!* And her father was dead!

'Poor Martin.'

Lucy looked at her mother and frowned. She had sounded sincere. *'Poor Martin?'*

'Yes. He tried to buy happiness. It doesn't work that way, Lucy. Happiness has to be worked at. No relationship is ever smooth, but a little give, a little take, a lot of loving, a lot of understanding, they all go to build up one perfect whole. If you love Conan, Lucy, don't hold what he's done against him. If he's half as good to you as Alan is to me, then I know you'll be happy. They're kind men, both of them. Conan's shrewd and sometimes ruthless, but most of it's a veneer, and certainly his heart is in the right place.'

Lucy thought a long time about what her mother had said. She was right, of course. Wasn't her mother always? She was a wise woman. She had experienced life at its best and at its worst. She had been devastated when her husband died, yet she still had this capacity for loving and forgiving. She was a gentle, compassionate person, and Lucy wished she could be more like her.

Not until after dinner did Lucy find herself alone with Conan again. All day she had felt his eyes on her, watching everything she did, making silent love to her, making her feel as though he were crawling beneath her skin and possessing her.

Consequently when her mother and Alan retired early to bed, announcing they were going to watch television for a while in their room, she found herself hungering to be held in his arms.

The sky had cleared now, as it so often did on an English evening, and they sat outside on the hammock, swinging idly, watching a blood-red sun slowly sink below the horizon. Conan said softly, 'I think we have some unfinished business?'

Without a word Lucy slid into his arms, and all the needs and desires that had played havoc with her all day were poured out into that kiss.

Up above them from the open window she heard her mother laugh, and she remembered her advice. *Don't hold what he's done against him.* 'I think,' she whispered in Conan's ear, when he eventually raised his mouth from hers, 'that I'd like to retract my notice. Maybe I was a little hasty.'

He moved his head so that he could see her face clearly. 'You've come to your senses? You've decided that you love me, after all?' There was a dawn of new happiness in his eyes.

'No,' she answered quickly, 'oh, I don't know. I just know that I want to be with you. Perhaps if you could bear with me for a while?'

The light faded. 'Lucy, I want an all-or-nothing commitment.'

'I'm trying, Conan, I'm trying,' she choked. 'Something my mother said made me realise that maybe I'm wrong to bear a grudge for so long, but I can't turn about just like that. I need time.'

'How much time?' There was a firmness to his lips now, a hint that he was not prepared to give her the breathing space she needed.

'A few weeks?' she suggested tentatively.

'I'll give you a month.'

Lucy closed her eyes. Was she out of her mind or wasn't she? Would it work? Did she really want it to? Did she love Conan, or were these feelings that tormented her body still nothing more than animal magnetism? Only time would tell. Four weeks, she had. Was it enough?

But when he kissed her again Lucy felt a contentment that she had not experienced since meeting him. Perhaps it would work, after all.

Certainly he went out of his way to make her fall in love with him. He wined and dined her, taking her to the most romantic little places. He showered her with gifts of jewellery and perfume. He bought her a book of love poems, a silver love spoon, a crystal bell with a pair of porcelain love birds perched on the top. He expressed his love in every way possible, and Lucy's antagonism faded further and further into the back of her mind.

Then, one night, as they were sitting sipping their coffee after a perfect night out at their favourite restaurant, he told her that he had given Martin Goodfellow a job.

Lucy could not believe it. She felt her happiness collapse and the fires of hell start up inside her all over again. 'How could you?' she flared. '*How could you?*

How can you trust him? Besides, he doesn't deserve a second chance.'

'*Lucy!*'

There was a warning note in his voice, but she ignored it. 'Have you forgotten what he did? It was his fault my father died. I——'

'I seem to remember you telling me it was mine,' he cut in coldly, and there was ice now in the depths of his eyes. Silver slivers that sliced right through her.

'It was both of you,' she fumed. 'And by giving him a job you're corroborating that fact. Oh, God, I wish I'd never met you.'

'You think I don't feel the same?' he snarled. 'I should have known from your attitude when we first met that the whole game was futile.'

'*Game?*' she shrieked, heedless of the curious glances of the other diners. 'Is that all it is to you?'

'It's what you've turned it into, you and your bigoted mind. A fiasco, a farce, a complete waste of time and effort. At least we now both know the truth. It wouldn't work. Not ever. If you want to put in your notice again, Lucy, that's fine by me. I don't want to see you again.'

He beckoned to the waiter for his bill and as soon as it was paid he stood up. 'Are you coming?'

'I'll take a taxi,' said Lucy stiffly. 'The feeling's mutual, you know. I don't want to see you, either. I shan't be in the office tomorrow. You can list me with all the other girls who've left because of you.'

His nostrils flared, and for just a minute Lucy thought he was going to strike her, then he turned and marched out of the restaurant, every line in his body shrieking aggression.

Lucy tilted her chin and stood up too, ignoring the now open curiosity at the other tables. She was too angry to feel embarrassed. The girl at the desk ordered her a taxi. Lucy heard the wild roar of Conan's car as he hurtled out of the car park at a dangerous speed. Serve him right if he gets himself killed, she thought viciously. She had been insane thinking it might work. For once her mother was wrong. She and Conan couldn't even be friends, let alone lovers.

Once home she went straight to her room, thankful that her mother and Alan were out. She could not have stood their questioning tonight.

When the phone rang she ignored it. Five minutes later it went again. She knew it was Conan and she did not want to speak to him. But when it rang a third time she knew that the only way to silence him was to answer. She snatched it up. 'I've got nothing else to say to you.'

'Is Mr Alan Templeton there?'

The strange male voice threw her.

'Hello? Mr Alan Templeton, please.'

Lucy swallowed and took hold of herself. 'I'm sorry, he's out. Can I give him a message?'

'Is that Mrs Templeton?'

'No, this is her daughter.'

'I'm afraid there's been an accident. Mr Conan Templeton. He's in hospital undergoing an emergency operation.'

Long after the police sergeant had rung off, Lucy held on to the receiver. Conan was hurt. He was in hospital. Dying! And it was all her fault. She must go to him. Now. He had been speeding because of her. *'Oh, Conan,'* she cried in silent anguish. *'What have I done to you?'*

She left a note for her mother and Alan—she could not wait for them to come back from wherever they had gone—and got out her car. The hospital he had been taken to was in Watford, though goodness knew what he was doing there. Presumably he had wanted to put as much distance between them as possible.

She drove at breakneck speed, unconscious that it was probably this very same urgency that had caused Conan's accident. All she knew was that she must get to him. She wanted to be there when he came round.

At the hospital she was told that a Dr Teal would like to speak to her before she saw Conan, and Lucy feared the worst. She was kept waiting for what seemed like hours, and yet in fact was only ten minutes.

'Miss Anderson?' A tall, vital man in his mid-fifties, with crisp, greying hair, held out his hand.

She nodded, liking the strength of him. He radiated confidence.

'You're Conan Templeton's stepsister, is that right?'

'Yes,' whispered Lucy painfully, 'and a very close friend.'

The doctor seemed to understand. 'And his father, has he been told?'

'I left a note. Both he and my mother were out, and I've no idea where they've gone or when they'll be back. I couldn't wait. I had to come, I was so afraid. How is he? Can I see him? What happened? What's wrong with him? Oh dear, it's all my fault.' Ready tears filled her eyes and the doctor gently took her hands and urged her into a seat.

'Nothing is your fault, my dear. Why do say that?'

'Because we'd had an argument and he walked out on me. I said some hurtful things and——'

'And now you're feeling as guilty as hell?' His blue eyes were kind and steady. 'Don't blame yourself. Accidents happen.'

Lucy swallowed a lump as big as a golfball in her throat. 'How badly is he hurt?'

'He's in intensive care, as you know, and he's not conscious yet, but he's young and strong and I'm——'

He was telling her nothing. It must be bad. 'Oh, God,' she cried, 'what will I do if he dies?'

The doctor touched her hand. 'It's our job to see that he doesn't.'

'Can I see him?'

He nodded. 'But I feel I must warn you he's not a pretty sight. I don't want you getting any more upset.'

'I'll try,' she whispered.

When she saw Conan, Lucy was glad Dr Teal had warned her. It was impossible to identify the man who lay there. His head and eyes were swathed in bandages. There were bruises and lacerations on the rest of his face, one cheek swollen grotesquely. One arm was bandaged and lay on top of the covers, and goodness knew what else was wrong with him. There were tubes and wires all over the place, and every breath was being monitored.

Lucy's eyes were wide when she had finished taking it all in. This was Conan? Conan, who was powerful and strong and virile, and indestructible, she had always thought. Reduced to an inert, unrecognisable form. Tears welled and flooded over, and the attendant nurse helped her into a chair by the bed.

'Conan?' Lucy whispered, touching his hand.

The nurse looked at her sympathetically. 'He's not come round from the anaesthetic yet.'

'But I can stay here?' she implored.

'Of course,' agreed the girl. 'Would you like a cup of tea?'

Lucy nodded.

'Oh, Conan,' whispered Lucy, as soon as she was on her own. 'I love you.' And this was the truth. She knew it now beyond any shadow of doubt. 'I love you. Please don't die. Please get better. I need you. If you die I shan't want to live either. You're my whole life. You're all I want—for ever.'

It had been futile bearing resentment over something that was not entirely Conan's fault. She didn't deserve him. He had been patient for so long—and Conan wasn't always a patient man.

The nurse returned and Lucy sipped the hot, sweet tea, never taking her eyes for one instant off Conan. He didn't stir. He hardly seemed to be breathing. Lucy was terrified.

How long she sat there she had no idea, but eventually Dr Teal appeared at her side. 'I think you ought to go up to the canteen and get something to eat.'

Lucy shook her head strongly. 'I won't leave him.'

'He doesn't know you're here. It will make no difference.'

'I don't care, I'm going to stay.'

And no amount of persuasion on his part would make her move.

More time passed, and then the door opened gently and Alan stepped inside. He looked tired and anguished, and his eyes shot from Lucy to the unconscious figure of his son, a silent question in their aching depths.

'He's not come round yet,' she said. 'I'm glad you're here. I'm desperately worried. How long do these things take?'

Alan pulled up another chair and took her hands in his. 'I've no idea.'

And in that instant Conan moved. Lucy thought it was a miracle. His arm shifted on the bed cover and his lips worked as though he was talking, but his mouth was dry and what he said was so faint neither of them could hear.

The nurse came to him and spoke. 'Mr Templeton? Mr Templeton, can you hear me?'

He made another movement and she looked pleased. 'That's good. It's all right, Mr Templeton, you can go back to sleep now.' She smiled at Lucy and Alan. 'He's out of the anaesthetic. I'll fetch Dr Teal.'

Lucy clung to Alan's hand, but neither one of them spoke. There was nothing they could say. They both loved this man who lay there fighting for his life.

The doctor arrived and checked for himself that everything was in order, and then he turned to Lucy and Alan. 'Mr Templeton, I think you ought to take this girl home and make her sleep. I don't want another patient on my hands.'

'I can't leave him,' she wailed.

'The doctor's right,' said Alan. 'You look all-in, Lucy. But I'd like a word with you privately, Doctor, before we leave.'

Dr Teal nodded and the two men left the room. Lucy sat on, staring at the bandaged figure. It was hard to imagine that this was Conan, that this was the man who had devastated her from the moment they first met. Why were they hiding him beneath these bandages? Exactly what had happened to him? Why wouldn't someone tell her?

Alan returned and, taking her arm, propelled her from the room. She fought him every inch of the way, looking longingly at Conan all the time.

'I won't go home,' she cried. 'It's too far. I'll book into a hotel. I can't leave Conan, Alan. It's my fault he's here.'

'Dr Teal told me something about that,' he said quietly. 'But you can't blame yourself, Lucy. He always did drive too fast. It could have happened at any time.'

Those famous words rang in Lucy's brain. It was what her mother had said about her father. But it wouldn't have happened, it wouldn't, not if she hadn't laid into him. 'Will you stay with me?' she asked chokingly.

Alan nodded. 'Try keeping me away. But there's no need to use a hotel. I have a house not far from here. At least, it was mine; it's Conan's now. I expect that's where he was heading.'

His admission surprised Lucy, though it shouldn't have done. There was still a lot she did not know about Conan. But at this moment she was more interested in his health than anything else. 'Did the doctor tell you how it happened and how badly he's hurt? He wouldn't tell me anything. Oh, Alan, he's not going to die, is he?' She forgot she was talking to Conan's father, that he would be hurt as much as she if Conan died.

'Conan's strong, he'll pull through,' said the older man confidently. 'And I'll tell you as much as I know once we're settled for the night.'

'Why hasn't my mother come?' frowned Lucy.

He grimaced wryly. 'She said that two tearful females would be more than I could handle. To tell you the truth, Lucy, I feel like crying myself.'

Lucy felt better, hearing Alan admit this. Men were always so good at hiding their feelings that she somehow never thought of them wanting to cry.

Silence settled over them as they made their short journey, each with their own private thoughts, their fears and hopes. Lucy offered up a prayer for Conan's recovery. She was desperately worried. It might not be so bad if she could see his face properly; it could be anyone.

How did she know it was Conan? His features were so distorted that it was impossible to recognise him. They were foolish thoughts, though. She knew it was Conan. She could feel and sense it, even if he wasn't instantly identifiable.

They arrived at the large, rambling house set in its own grounds, and Alan poured them both a brandy. Lucy sipped hers gratefully, feeling it warm and settle her stomach. 'Tell me what the doctor said. Is Conan really going to be all right? He doesn't look it to me.'

'To be honest with you, Lucy, the doctors don't know either. It's too early to say whether there'll be any permanent damage. They had to operate on his brain to stop internal bleeding. He was barely conscious when he was pulled out of the wreckage.' There was pain on Alan's face as he spoke.

'Damage to what?' frowned Lucy.

'His optic nerves. They fear for his sight.'

*'Oh, no!'* She clapped her hands to her mouth and looked at him in horror.

Alan nodded, swallowing hard, a muscle jerking in his jaw.

Lucy felt every part of her curling up in protest. Conan blind? No! No! *No!* 'But they don't know for certain?' It was an anguished whisper.

'No, they don't. And Dr Teal told me to look on the bright side.'

She nodded, her face devoid of all colour. 'That's easier said than done. Why did he have to tell you if he wasn't sure?' She could see now why he hadn't told her.

'Because I demanded to know everything.'

'His other injuries, they will heal?'

'Cuts and bruises, that's all. Nothing internal, thank God.'

'It will kill him if he goes blind,' she said achingly. 'He'll hate it. Oh, Alan, why did it have to happen to Conan?' She could not stop the tears racing down her cheeks now, and Alan gave her his handkerchief, holding her, offering her all the comfort he could. And perhaps he in his turn was deriving some comfort from her. They were two people sharing a common grief.

'How did the accident happen?' she ventured at length. 'Was anyone else hurt?' She had been so busy thinking about Conan and herself that she had given no thought to the fact that there might be someone else suffering besides themselves.

Alan looked grim. 'A car shot out of a side road in front of him. Brake failure, apparently. There was no way Conan could miss him, and the other driver never stood a chance.'

'You mean he's—dead?'

Her stepfather nodded.

Lucy closed her eyes and a shudder racked through her. It could have been Conan. So easily it could have been him. But at least he was alive, and what the hell did it matter if he never saw again or if his face was disfigured? Even if it had been his legs and he never walked again, what was that compared to losing your life? He was lucky in that respect.

It was a long time before they went to bed, Lucy reluctantly taking the sleeping pill the doctor had given Alan for her. 'I'll wake you if there's any news,' he promised. But morning came and the hospital hadn't been in touch, and when Alan phoned they said there was no change.

During the next few days they spent hours sitting at Conan's bedside, even though he was still heavily sedated and unaware of their presence. Then one morning they arrived at the intensive care unit and he wasn't there. The bed was empty. Lucy turned shocked eyes up to Alan, one thought only in her mind. *Conan was dead.* He had died during the night. Why hadn't someone told them? Why had they let them walk in here and find out for themselves?

But before she could speak a smiling nurse appeared. 'You'll be pleased to know Mr Templeton's off the critical list. He's been moved into a private ward.'

Lucy could not describe the feeling of relief that washed over her. Alan took her hand and squeezed it tightly as they followed the nurse, and she guessed that he had been thinking the same thing.

Conan still lay on his back, his eyes covered by the inevitable bandages, but there was no longer that deathly stillness about him. The swelling had gone down, and apart from the multi-coloured bruising and the purple lacerations, he was very recognisable. He had always had a strong mouth and jawline, and nothing had detracted from that.

Lucy went up to the bed and laid her own hand over his. 'Conan, it's me.' There was a break in her voice no matter how much she tried to tell herself to be strong. He wouldn't want tears. 'Welcome back to the land of the living.' She tried to inject humour into her tone.

He tensed. 'What are *you* doing here?'

Her face creased with pain. 'I've been here every day. How are you feeling?'

'Like hell,' he growled, and moved his hand from beneath hers.

Alan joined Lucy at the bedside. 'Son?'

'Father? You're here, too? Come to see the bruised and battered body, eh?' A derisive smile curved his lips.

'At least I have one up on you; I can't see what I look like.'

Lucy winced, and wondered whether they had told him there was a danger he could lose his sight. She hoped not. She couldn't see Conan accepting it. And they might be wrong. She prayed they were.

Alan clasped his son's hand. 'You've given us all a fright.'

'No bigger than the one I got when that idiot drove straight out in front of me.' Conan moved his head angrily, then winced in pain.

'Steady, darling,' said Lucy gently, the endearment slipping out without her realising it.

'Don't fuss,' he snarled.

Then the nurse came over and asked them to leave, a bristling elderly woman who had been sitting in a corner of the room watching them closely.

'But we've only just got here,' protested Lucy.

'We can't have Conan getting excited,' said the woman. 'Not at this stage.'

'I promise we won't say anything more to upset him.'

But the nurse was adamant. 'You can come back after lunch.'

They walked in the hospital grounds, they drank cup after cup of coffee, they attempted to eat a cheese sandwich, but all the time they looked at their watches. Lucy could not hide her hurt. 'Conan doesn't want me,' she said tearfully.

'Nonsense. You had a tiff, but once he's feeling better you'll soon sort yourselves out.'

'I love him,' she whispered, her eyes wide green pools of anguish.

Alan smiled. 'And Conan loves you, I'm sure. I've never seen him look at any other girl the way he does you.'

'Not even Norma?' she asked with a wintry smile.

'You know about her?'

'He told me.'

'Not even Norma,' he confirmed. 'Be patient, be tolerant, don't let him get you down, and all will be well, I'm certain of it.'

At two o'clock they presented themselves back in Conan's room. A different nurse was in attendance this time, young and pleasant. 'I'm glad you're here, Mr Templeton,' she said. 'He's becoming impossible. You look as though you'll be able to keep him in order.'

Alan grinned. 'I lost control of my son a long time ago, but I'll do my best.'

'We don't want him getting agitated,' said the nurse, suddenly serious. 'His head's still giving him a great deal of pain, and the calmer he is, the better it will be for him.'

'Stop talking about me as though I'm not here,' barked Conan.

Alan strode over to him and clasped his hand between both of his. 'It's good to see you getting better, son. We'll have you out of here in no time at all.'

'If you don't, I'll discharge myself,' warned Conan. 'And when are they going to take these damn bandages off?' He brushed his hand across his eyes. 'What the hell's wrong with me? Do you know? No one will tell me. Have they told you?'

'Patience, son,' said Alan steadily. 'You got pretty badly knocked about. You don't walk out of a collision like that without a scratch.'

'Where's Lucy, is she still here?'

Alan smiled and beckoned her towards him. 'Of course she is. Try keeping her away.'

'I don't want her here. Hasn't she got the message yet? It's all over between us.'

Lucy felt ready tears spring to her eyes. It wasn't over, not by a long chalk. 'Conan,' she said feverishly, 'I didn't mean what I said. I'm sorry. I've been a fool.'

'Don't tell me something I already know,' he derided.

'I love you,' she rushed on, 'I really do. It's taken this to make me realise how mistaken I've been, but now I want to make amends. I want to beg your forgiveness. Oh, Conan, I love you so much.' She took hold of his hand and pressed it to her lips, and her hot tears scalded him. When Alan silently moved away she did not even notice.

The silence lengthened while Conan seemed to be grappling with an inner conflict. The minutes stretched on and on. Then, when Lucy began to despair, he groaned and, hooking his hand behind her head, he brought her mouth fiercely down on his. It was the sweetest kiss Lucy had ever tasted.

'I wouldn't recommend this sort of measure to win a girl's heart,' he said with wry humour, 'but if it's done the trick I reckon it's all going to be worth while.'

'It's all my fault, Conan,' she said tearfully. 'What can I say? What can I do?'

'Kiss me again,' he muttered thickly. 'Feed me the love I need. You've no idea how deranged I felt when I walked out of that restaurant.'

When their lips met Lucy's heart pounded, and she wondered whether it was good for him, because surely he must be experiencing these same emotions?

Suddenly he went limp beneath her, and what little colour he had drained from him. Lucy sat up and he put his hand to his head. The nurse came across. 'Are you in pain again, Conan?'

'Yes, dammit.'

'I think you'd better leave,' she said to Lucy. 'I'll give him something to make him sleep. Come back tomorrow. He'll be feeling better then.'

'I don't want Lucy to go.'

'But Mr Templeton——'

'I want her to stay here.'

'Very well,' humoured the young nurse, grimacing at Lucy. 'I'll give you something to ease the pain, but I want you to lie very still and very quiet. No more kissing your visitor.'

'If I want to kiss Lucy I damn well will,' he snarled.

Lucy decided he must be feeling better than he looked if he could speak to the nurse like this. And the nurse was apparently used to such obstreperous patients, because she merely smiled as she put an injection into his arm. To the watchful Lucy it seemed like only seconds before his eyelids drooped and he fell asleep.

She joined Alan outside and smiled shyly. 'I'm afraid we'll have to go, the nurse has put him to sleep. He was getting too excited for his own good.'

'I take it he accepted your apology?'

Lucy nodded.

Alan turned and hugged her. 'I'm happy for you, Lucy. And for my son.'

As each day passed Conan grew progressively fitter. He was sitting up now when they arrived, and the dressings had been removed apart from those covering his eyes. They had shaved his head when they operated, but his hair was already beginning to grow back, and Lucy did not dare tell him how funny he looked.

Alan went home to spend a few days with Valerie, promising to bring her with him the next time, but Lucy would not budge. The nurses got Conan out of bed to walk each day, and Lucy hung on to his arm to guide him round his room and along the corridors, and she never ceased to tell him how much she loved him. So much time had been lost, she had so much to make up.

He grew increasingly irritable and sometimes he snapped at her and told her he didn't want her to come again, but the next second he would apologise. 'I'd go out of my mind if you didn't come. This is a hell-hole of a place. I'll be all right when they take these damn bandages off.'

'Have they said anything about when it will be?' she asked timidly. It was a subject she had been afraid to broach.

He smiled. 'Tomorrow. And then, my beautiful Lucy, I'll be able to see you again. Kiss me. Let me feel you. Oh, God, you smell good.'

And he felt good in her arms.

Alan phoned that night and she told him that tomorrow was the testing day. 'I'll come down,' he said at once.

'And bring Mom?'

'Yes, she's missing her daughter.'

But when Lucy arrived at the hospital the following day her worst fears were realised. Conan could not see. Dr Teal stopped her on her way in to him and told her the grim news. 'I'm so sorry.'

Lucy felt a lump rise in her throat. 'How's Conan taking it?'

The doctor grimaced. 'He's called us all swines and various other words I would not like to repeat.'

'That sounds like Conan,' she said. 'Can I go in?'

He nodded. 'Take care. He's feeling very sorry for himself and he's quite likely to take it out on you.'

'I don't think so,' she smiled, confident now in their relationship.

She walked into his ward and he sat there in dark glasses, and when he heard her footsteps he stiffened. She crossed to his bed and kissed him as she always did, and there was no response.

'Hey, Conan, it's me. The love of your life.'

Still no response.

'Aren't you going to speak to me?'

'Have they told you?' he asked abruptly, and the dull tones of his voice gave away his anguish.

'Yes,' she admitted quietly, 'but it's not the end of the world, Conan.'

'What the hell good am I without eyes?' he said harshly. 'Why didn't they let me die? And you can get out of my life, Lucy, because I'm no good to you, either.' He thrust her savagely from him.

'Conan—please—you don't know what you're saying. It's been a shock, I know, but once you get used to the idea, you'll feel differently. I love you. This makes no difference. I don't care that you can't see. I will be your eyes. I will——'

'Lucy.' His voice was loud now in the tiny room. 'Lucy, I meant what I said. Now get out, and don't let me see you——' he checked himself disgustedly '—don't come near me again.'

# CHAPTER EIGHT

LUCY could not believe that Conan did not want to see her again. Because he had gone blind he wanted her out of his life? Why? Surely he needed her more than ever?

'Conan,' she said persuasively, 'please don't say that. This makes no difference. I love you so much I don't care whether——'

'I mean it, Lucy.' There was a hard note in his voice that was new.

'No, you don't,' she protested, trying to keep her tone light. 'You'll soon realise that——'

'That I'm no good to anybody,' he cut in fiercely. 'Can you just picture me stumbling and fumbling and generally making a fool of myself? And you think I want you to be witness to that? No, thank you, Lucy.'

'So what the hell will you do with yourself?' She felt herself growing as angry as Conan.

'I don't know yet. Go home and learn to cope, I suppose.'

'On your own?'

'I'll manage.'

'I want to help you, Conan.' A note of pleading crept into Lucy's voice.

*'No!'* He said the word loudly, like the crack of a whip, and Lucy jumped. 'I don't need you, or want you. You and I are finished. I should never have taken you back.'

Hot tears ran down her cheeks. How could he do this to her? Wasn't his love strong enough to withstand this set-back? 'Please, Conan,' she whispered. He had chased her so long and so hard in the first place that surely he couldn't seriously want to cast her out his life now?

His voice roared and echoed round the corners of the room. *'Get out, and don't come back.'*

Lucy had never heard such anger. She felt as though she were being physically struck. His whole body was rigid, veins stood out on his brow, and he kept smashing his fist down on the bed.

She knew that if she didn't go now, if she tried again to touch him, to plead with him, to persuade him, he would lose control. Blinded by her tears, she swung round, and bumped straight into Alan was who standing just inside the room.

He gathered her to him and she didn't have to tell him what was happening because he had witnessed the ugly scene himself. 'You'd better go,' he said softly. 'Your mother's outside in my car. Go to her and I'll see you in a minute.'

But Lucy did not want to see her mother, not yet; she needed a few minutes to herself. She sat down on a chair in the corridor. Perhaps Alan would talk some sense into him? Perhaps once Conan had accepted his blindness he would want to see her again? He needed her. Why couldn't he see that? She would help him. She would devote her whole life to him. It made not the slightest bit of difference. He was still Conan. He was still the same man, the man she loved, the man she wanted to marry, whose children she wanted to bear.

The low murmur of voices in Conan's room suddenly rose to a crescendo of angry tones. Lucy sat on the edge of her seat, wondering whether to go in and interrupt. Then Alan came out, red-faced and furious. He glanced at Lucy, surprised to see her still there. 'Come on, let's get out of here.'

'But Conan—he might—perhaps I ought to——'

'Conan wants no one at this moment, especially not you,' he said firmly. 'He has to work this thing out for himself, and from what I've just seen it's going to take a hell of a long time.'

Lucy trailed him reluctantly out to his car. Her mother kissed her, but refrained from asking any questions, seeing by their faces that there was something seriously wrong, and knowing they would tell her in their own good time.

'I'll follow you,' said Alan.

During the short drive, Lucy could not dismiss from her mind's eye the picture of Conan as she had last seen him. He was angry, hurt, disappointed, bitter, all these things and more. It was the hardest blow of his life and it was going to take him a long time to come to terms with it. But he would, eventually, she felt sure, and then he would take back all that he had said. They would get married and she would give him all the help and guidance that she could until he became as independent as it was possible for a blind person to be.

By the time they reached the house Alan had told Valerie the bad news and she gathered her daughter to her. 'Look on the bright side, love. It might not be permanent. These doctors don't know everything.'

'It's not me you should be telling,' she said through her tears, 'it's Conan.'

Her mother grimaced. 'From what Alan's told me, Conan's feeling pretty sorry for himself, lashing out at whoever goes near. It's understandable, though. When your father died I could have screamed every time anyone offered me sympathy. I wanted Eric back, not meaningless condolences. I imagine that's how Conan's feeling, as though part of him has died too. He'll get over it in time. You'll have to be patient.'

'He says he doesn't want anything to do with me ever again.'

Valerie Anderson nodded. 'I know, but I shouldn't take it too much to heart. Give him a few days to adjust and you'll find that nothing's changed.'

But in this Valerie was wrong. Lucy visited Conan regularly, and just as regularly he sent her away. 'For pity's sake, when are you going to get it into your thick skull that we're finished?' he demanded savagely. 'You're wasting your time coming here. You're wasting your breath talking to me.'

There was never any let-up. He wouldn't even let her touch him. Whenever she laid her hand on his he knocked it away, and she didn't dare try to kiss him. It was breaking her up, if he only knew it, but when she said she loved him he wouldn't listen.

'I thought you loved me too,' she reproached. 'I don't see how losing your sight can make you love me any the less.'

'You wouldn't have any idea what it's like,' he thrust scathingly, his fingers clenching and unclenching, his jaw grim. He never smiled these days. He was always uptight. She despaired of ever seeing the old Conan again. He spoke of going away, right away from everyone he knew, everyone who loved him. He was so bitter, it was unbelievable.

'I don't think I can take much more of this,' Lucy said to her mother. 'I wonder if he knows how much he's hurting me?'

'He knows, all right,' said Valerie. 'He's using you as his whipping post. If you want my advice, keep well away from him for a while.'

'But then he'll think I'm deserting him, he'll think that I'm turned off by his blindness.'

'He knows that's not true.'

'But he's so irrational these days that I never know what he's thinking.'

'That's why you need to give yourself a breathing space. He needs time to come to terms with himself. I think we should all go back to Derby and let him get on with his life the way he wants to. For a while, at least.'

'No!' Lucy was insistent. 'You and Alan can go, but I shall stay here.'

Alan added his persuasions to Valerie's. 'I know he's my son, and I love him dearly, but this is one of those occasions when it's best to harden your heart. I don't want to leave him any more than you do, but we're doing no good. He's made up his mind that he doesn't want us, and for the time being I think it's best if we go along with that.'

Tears began to roll down Lucy's cheeks, silent, un-bidden tears. They tasted salty on her lips and she dashed them away with the back of her hand. Neither of them had any idea what they were asking of her. She loved Conan more than she had ever thought possible. It was futile suggesting she desert him. 'You two go,' she said, her voice choked with the pain of Conan's rejection, 'but I can't.'

'It won't help him,' said Valerie sadly.

'I'll not visit him, I'll leave him alone for a while and see what happens. But wild horses won't drag me away from here. I shall keep in touch with the hospital and get a day-to-day bulletin on his progress.'

Alan looked at his wife. 'Your daughter's very stubborn.'

Valerie smiled. 'Don't I know it?'

And so Lucy's mother and Alan went back to Derby and Lucy stayed on in Conan's house, phoning the hospital every day, sometimes going there hoping to catch a glimpse of Conan, but never managing to do so.

A week later she walked into his ward, deciding she had left him alone long enough. Apart from the fact that he wore dark glasses, there looked nothing wrong with him. His hair was growing fast and the pallor that had haunted his first days had now gone. He sat in a chair near the window, and if Lucy had not known he was blind she would have thought he was looking outside.

She had tried to imagine what he must be experiencing. She had walked round and round his house with her eyes closed, she had attempted doing all the ordinary mundane tasks and discovered how difficult it was, how much she relied on her eyes, and she realised how hard it was going to be for him. More difficult than for some people, because Conan was an arrogant, proud man who could not easily accept help. He would want to do everything for himself, even if it were impossible.

Suddenly he turned his head and she could have sworn he was looking directly at her. Her heart gave an enormous leap. Perhaps a miracle had happened? But his next words told her differently. 'Who's there? Florence, is that you?'

Who was Florence? wondered Lucy. She said nothing, not sure what to say, not sure what sort of a welcome she would get, if any. He might tell her to go to hell. On the other hand he might be glad she was here. Perhaps he had missed her? Lucy hoped so, she really did. She had wanted to ask the nurse whether Conan ever mentioned her, but he was alone. It seemed cruel to leave him. He needed company, someone to talk to, someone to take his mind off his problems.

As she moved towards him Lucy put herself into Conan's shoes, listening to the sounds she made, the soft pad of her sandals, the rustle of her skirt. She had never taken any notice of these sort of things before. But she could see that Conan was listening, and she wanted to hear what he heard.

'Lucy?'

Now how could he have known it was her? She could have been a nurse, the unknown Florence, anyone. What had given her away?

'Lucy, is that you?' His tone was clipped and impatient.

She took a breath and held it, and then said softly, 'Yes, Conan, it's me. How did you know?'

For an instant there was a glimmer of something in his eyes, a memory, a happy thought, then the mask was on again and his voice was cold. 'Your perfume.'

It was a simple statement of fact. He had always said how much he liked her to wear this particular brand, that it excited him and made him want her, that he had known other girls who used it but it smelled better on her, more sensual, more erotic, arousing all his emotions.

And yet she hadn't given it a thought as she walked across the room. She was so used to the smell herself that she was not even aware of it. Not that it was doing her much good today. It was evident by his attitude that he had not had a change of heart. A sudden heaviness settled over her.

But deliberately she made her tone light. 'Hi, punk, how're you doing?'

He immediately touched a hand to his hair and a muscle jerked in his jaw. In other circumstances he would have laughed and joked with her. Now he didn't think it was funny. 'How do you think I'm doing?' he demanded. 'Bloody awful, and I don't need you around to witness it.'

Lucy tried to ignore the harshness of his tone. 'Still on that tack, I see. I thought you might have come to your senses.'

*'Senses?'* he roared. 'Goddammit, Lucy, I lose my sight and you think I shouldn't let it bother me.'

'Conan, please——' She touched her hand to his arm, but he knocked it cruelly away. She clenched her teeth and moved a few inches from him. 'You're behaving like a child.'

He did not answer. His head was turned once again to the window, his shoulders solid and stiff through the black silk of his pyjamas.

'You're hurting yourself, not me.'

His fingers strummed on the window sill.

'You're making things worse,'

He turned at that. 'And how do you work that out, Miss Know-It-All?'

'Because you're shutting yourself away,' she said, trying to keep her voice calm. 'And for what reason? Do you think because you've lost your sight it makes you some kind of a freak?'

'It means I can't do all the things that I used to do.'

'Hell, Conan,' she said impatiently, 'the world's full of blind people all leading a normal life.'

'Normal for whom?' he demanded.

'You have to learn to adapt.'

'So everyone keeps telling me. I've been counselled and talked to and advised and preached at until I'm sick and fed up of the whole damn thing.'

'Dr Teal says you'll be going home soon.'

'To what? A life of darkness.'

'At least you do have a life to lead. The guy you hit is dead.'

It was a cruel taunt when the accident had been the other man's fault. But Lucy felt it needed to be said. She had to snap Conan out of this self-pitying state.

His fingers curled into fists, his knuckles gleaming white. 'Get out of here, Lucy.'

But for once she was determined not to be intimidated. 'I love you, Conan.'

A muscle jerked again in his jaw. 'Go and find someone else to love.'

'I only want you.'

'Where's my father?'

She smiled at the way he had neatly changed the subject. 'At home with my mother. He thinks you're being irrational too.'

'So why the hell didn't you go with them?'

'They wanted me to, but my place is here.'

He snorted derisively. 'You're not married to me, I don't own you, you're free to go. I don't want you feeling obliged. I'll manage. I know I've said some pretty stupid things, but I'll get used to it. I'll have to.' This last was added with a note of savagery.

'I'm also free to stay,' Lucy said quietly. 'And I'm not doing it out of any sense of pity. I've told you, I love you. I want to marry you. You're never going to get rid of me.'

In response, he turned his head away and for a long time there was silence in the room. Lucy watched him. He was angry, but whether with her or himself she did not know. She ached to hold him, to feel his arms about her, to share his hurt and their love, to face the future together. She wished he wouldn't shut her out.

The door suddenly opened and a pretty young nurse came in. Lucy had turned to see who it was; now she looked back at Conan and saw that he too was alert to another person in the room.

He listened intently as she crossed towards him. 'Florence?'

'Julie,' the nurse amended.

'But Florence suits you better,' he insisted.

'After Florence Nightingale,' she explained to Lucy, with a faintly embarrassed smile. 'I'm sure I'm nothing like her.'

'You're a good nurse. You look after my every need. Isn't that enough?'

Lucy wondered whether the emphasis was intentional. She looked sharply at the nurse's face. Julie was smiling softly, her fingers already on his wrist, her eyes on her watch.

It amazed her that he had recognised this nurse before she had spoken. Did she have her own distinctive smell too, or was it the way she walked, her particular foot-steps? Being blind must awaken senses that sighted people did not use.

'Mmm.' The nurse frowned. 'Your pulse is a little fast, Conan. Let's take your blood pressure.'

He was relaxed with the girl, smiling even, seeming to like her touching him, and Lucy noticed that his hand was on her arm as she worked. Perhaps he needed the reassurance, perhaps he needed to feel people now he could no longer see, but whatever it was, it ignited a flare of jealousy inside Lucy. He didn't want to touch her, so why was he making up to this strange girl? Was it really all over between them?

His blood pressure was up too. 'What have you been doing?' Julie asked, grinning all over her face. 'Or need I ask. This is your girlfriend, isn't it?'

'My ex-girlfriend,' growled Conan.

'And I'm just leaving.' There was a catch in Lucy's voice which she hoped he had not heard. 'Goodbye, Conan.'

He did not respond and Lucy did not look back. She did not want to see him smiling and talking so easily to Julie.

By the time she reached her car her eyes had filled with tears, and she sat for a few minutes until she was capable of driving.

At home, Lucy wandered through the rooms like someone lost. She could not make up her mind what to do. Whether to hang around until Conan was discharged and hope things would work out, or whether to go home, go somewhere, anywhere, so long as it was nowhere near him.

Conan had made it perfectly clear he wanted her out of his life, but she could not be certain that he meant it. Once he had come to terms with his blindness he might feel differently. He still loved her, she felt sure. It was his pride that had taken the worst beating of all.

For three more days she stayed, wondering, hoping, praying. And then one morning Dr Teal phoned to say that Conan had been discharged. 'In fact he's on his way there now,' he added.

Lucy was staggered. 'I wish you'd let me know. I would have come and fetched him.'

She had built up quite a rapport with the doctor, and he knew exactly what was going on between her and Conan. What was more, he understood. She could almost see him smiling. 'Conan thinks he's going home to an empty house. You still haven't told him you're staying there?'

'No,' she admitted.

'He needs you, Lucy, whether he knows it or not. Don't let him get you down.'

'I'll try,' she agreed, but knew it was easier said than done. Conan had always been very much in charge of himself and his life, and he could not bear the thought of her watching his efforts to adapt to his blindness.

When she saw the taxi pull up Lucy's heart began to pound. She was not sure now whether to go out and guide him in or let him find his own way. But even as she watched a nurse climbed out of the taxi and turned to help. It was Julie. Florence Nightingale. The Lady of the Lamp.

Lucy's spirits dropped.

But when Conan walked through the door he was alone. He stood there, uncertain, unaware of her presence, trying to get the feel of the place that he knew so well and yet was now strange to him.

There would be all sorts of obstacles to overcome. Lucy wanted to go to him, lead him forward, guide him around, explain, warn. But he would not allow that, she knew. He had to work things out for himself.

'Hello, Conan,' she said quietly, realising that she must make her presence known.

He swore explosively. 'Dammit, Lucy, what are you doing here?'

She swallowed hard. 'This is where I've been staying. I decided you needed me.'

'Like hell I do.' His mouth was grim, his jaw clenched. 'I'll work this thing out on my own or not at all.'

'It will be easier with someone to help you. Please let me stay, Conan.' He looked as though he had lost weight.

His cheek bones were more prominent than they had been, his face was all angles and hard, uncompromising lines. He looked fierce and somehow menacing behind his dark glasses.

'No!' He took a step towards the sound of her voice and almost cannoned into her, but his hand closed unerringly over her shoulder, his long, strong fingers biting deeply into her flesh. 'I want you to go,' he hissed fiercely.

'But who will help you?' Lucy could not bring herself to walk out. 'There's no one here, you might——'

'I want no one,' he grated. 'I have a lot of learning to do, Lucy, and I intend doing it in private. So get the hell out of here.'

'Don't you ever want to see me again?' Was that really her voice, that thin, pleading wail?

'Never. It's over.'

'Don't you love me any more?'

His head jerked. 'What I feel doesn't enter into it. I'm a changed man, Lucy. I'm not the man you fell in love with.' His lips twisted bitterly and there was cold contempt on his face. For her? Or for himself? She did not know.

'But I am the same girl,' she said strongly, and with sudden courage lifted her arms and put her hands behind his head, turning up her face and kissing him full on the mouth, arching her body against him, letting him see that nothing had changed so far as she was concerned.

She put every ounce of feeling into that kiss, and was just on the verge of withdrawing, realising it was getting her nowhere, that she had made a mistake in thinking she could arouse him, in believing that she could rekindle the flame that had once burned so strongly inside him, when with a groan his arms went around her.

His mouth clamped over hers in a kiss so merciless it was frightening. It bruised and punished as though he was trying to expurgate himself of all the desires and passion that had built up during the weeks he was in hospital.

He ground her lips back against her teeth as he tried to deepen the kiss. There was none of the gentleness that Lucy normally associated with Conan. This was raw sex, pure animal hunger, a desire to take what was being offered, to use her for his own gratification.

He tore off his glasses, his hand coming up behind her head, imprisoning it, making it impossible for her to move.

Noises of protest came from deep in Lucy's throat and she pounded her fists against him, but he was rock hard and invincible. Within seconds her hands were held firmly behind her back while his other hand took hold of her jaw, trying to force her to submit.

She did not want him to kiss her like this, she did not want to be a sex object, she wanted him to love her tenderly, to treat her with the respect and courtesy that he had always shown.

Finally she had to gasp for air, and when she did so his tongue at last entered her bruised mouth, ravishing its softness and moistness so thoroughly that she felt faint. He was devouring her and she could taste his masculinity, and despite her fears and protests he overpowered her senses to such a degree that they whirled until she went dizzy.

Suddenly and abruptly, he jerked away. His sightless eyes were on her, and he frowned savagely as his hands clamped down on her shoulders in a grip that made her wince.

'How are you feeling now?' His mouth curled in contempt. 'Still desirous of my body, or has all that changed now you can see what I've turned into? If the accident has taught me nothing else, it's taught me what a tenuous hold we have on life. It's best to take what's offered and live each day as it comes. I have no intention of making any commitments.'

His hands left her shoulders to trail slowly down over the naked flesh of her shoulders, experimentally touching the shoelace-thin straps of her cotton top, acquainting himself with what she wore, discovering she was braless. And as his hands felt her softly swollen breasts their hardened peaks gave away the fact that she was very much aroused.

'But if you're still intent on—*welcoming*—me into my home,' he went on, with a bitter emphasis on the word welcome, 'then I think I shall enjoy it.'

Lucy swayed as she stood in front of Conan, knowing she ought to move, to deny herself him. He was a man with a mighty powerful need and he would take her and use her, not because she was Lucy, the girl he loved, but because she was a woman. Any woman would have done. Florence Nightingale. He might even have preferred her. And the nurse had definitely taken a fancy to him. It had been there in her eyes the day they met in the ward, and again today when she helped him out of the taxi. But no matter what thoughts raced through her mind, Lucy could not move. He meant too much to her, and his kiss, torturous though it had been, had aroused her to fever-pitch.

His contempt deepened. 'Do I take it that your silence means assent? Or do I have to find the answer for myself?' Before she could realise his intentions, he had snapped the shoestring straps and yanked down her cotton top.

Lucy gasped as his hands closed over her breasts, as his thumbs grazed her nipples, sending wave after wave of sheer sensation through her body. She closed her eyes and did not realise he had lowered his head until she felt the rasp of his tongue where his thumbs had once been.

She looked down and saw the blackness of his head and she closed her hands over it, moaning softly in the back of her throat, holding him against her. In her aroused state it did not seem to matter that he was using her. This was Conan, the man she loved, the man she wanted to marry. He had every right to her body and she could never turn him away.

He lifted his head and his mouth was twisted in anguish and his need of her was deep and dark in his unseeing eyes. 'Damn you, Lucy. Why did you have to be here?'

She realised that his anger was caused by his frustrated desire. His blood was pounding as much as hers, his hands shaking, there was a sheen of perspiration on his face. 'I thought you'd need me,' she whispered painfully. 'And I need you, Conan.'

A shudder racked right through him, and in the next instant Lucy found herself swept up in his arms. 'If you need me that much, then you can damn well have me.' He was going to take her to his bedroom! Alarm shot through her. What if he stumbled and fell, what if—— But the next instant he laid her on the floor and began to rip the rest of her clothes from her.

'If I can't bloody well make it upstairs, then we'll do it here.' Rage and passion and frustration conflicted on his face, and when he had stripped her naked he began to tear off his own clothes.

Lucy could only lie and watch, her eyes filling with tears, her whole body aching and wanting, and yet crying out against this cruel invasion. She ought to crawl away, but she was powerless. Her palms were clammy, her throat dry, and she could not control the wild trembling of her limbs.

He peeled off his shirt, pulled down the zip on his trousers and when he stood free the maleness of him was overpowering. His head was thrown back, his eyes closed as if in agony, his jaw dangerously clenched. Even his fingers were curled. He took several deep breaths, as if trying to control his anger, as if willing himself not to go through with it, and Lucy watched him, mesmerised.

The next moment he was down beside her on the carpet. 'There's no backing out now, Lucy,' he muttered, his voice thick with emotion.

Lucy did not want to back out. She met his kiss with a fierceness that matched his, her mouth open willingly now, offering all of herself to him. She would not let it be rape. He was taking her against his own will, not hers. She would show him that, she would respond in every way she knew how, and perhaps he would finally accept that she loved him exactly as he was.

She touched her fingers to his chest, thrilling to the sensation of his hair-roughened skin, then moved her palms slowly over his strong shoulders and the hard muscles in his back, feeling every part of him, luxuriating in their closeness. He was a warm, wonderful man, and she loved him deeply.

His hands captured her breasts, her nipples tortured between thumb and forefinger before he impatiently blazed a downward trail, finding the vulnerable heart of her and then thrusting her legs savagely apart with an urgent thigh.

Lucy's fingers fastened on his shoulders and she moaned and arched herself against him. His frenzy merely served to increase her own desire, and she lifted her hips to his as he moved over her.

There was a moment's blazing light in his eyes before he entered her, and Lucy enjoyed every second of his savage lovemaking, raking her fingers down his spine, crying her pleasure out aloud, matching the movements of his body with rhythms of her own.

A groan was wrenched from deep in his soul when it was finally over, a last vigorous movement that left her shaking and limp and gasping for air. She lay with her eyes closed, her mouth open, Conan's dead weight holding her down. He was utterly spent, his harsh breathing the only sound in the silent hall.

As the seconds ticked away and he did not move, Lucy wondered whether it hadn't been too much for him. His body was wet with perspiration, and after all he had only just been discharged from hospital. He had been critically ill. She oughtn't to have goaded him.

'Conan?' she ventured huskily.

He stirred and rolled off her, and the blazing hatred in his face made Lucy wince. *It hadn't helped.* Letting him make love to her had made no difference at all. Tears rolled freely down her cheeks and she snatched up her clothes and ran for the stairs.

His voice cracked through the air like a whip. 'While you're up there, Lucy, pack your bags. Nothing's changed. I don't need you any more.' His lips curled in contempt and derision. 'If you thought offering me your body would make a difference, well, it hasn't. Go away and don't attempt to get in touch with me again.'

# CHAPTER NINE

TEARS blinded Lucy's vision as she flung the few clothes her mother had brought down into her case. Uncontrollable sobs shook her shoulders. This was the end. She had tried and lost. Conan had decided that he no longer wanted or needed her in his life. It was hard to accept, even more difficult to gather her things together and walk out.

Lucy had never really believed he meant it. She had thought that when he left the hospital he would see things in a different light, he would realise that their love meant more than anything else in the world. Surely he didn't think that his blindness bothered her?

She paused in the act of pushing in her last pair of sandals. She simply couldn't walk out without having done everything possible to sustain their relationship. It had taken her so long to come to terms with the part Conan had played in their lives that she could not throw it all away, not without a fight. She would speak to him one more time.

Once her mind was made up her tears subsided. But just in case he could not be persuaded, she finished packing and snapped the locks. She hoped against hope, though, that in a few minutes she would be hanging her dresses up again. Somehow, some way, she had to make him see sense. He needed her, whether he knew it or not.

Hauling her case off the bed, Lucy looked sadly around the little guest-room she had been using, then she pulled open the door—and was shocked to see Conan standing there. Had he been about to enter? Had he come to say that he had changed his mind? Hope flooded through her.

He was dressed again now and there was nothing on his face to suggest that a love scene had just taken place. In fact, it was devoid of all emotion. He looked pale and tired, and she was worried about him.

'Conan?' Lucy's voice was a mere whisper. 'Are you all right?'

'Why the hell shouldn't I be?' he barked. 'I came to see what was taking you so long.'

She closed her eyes, feeling the optimism drain out of her. 'I've finished packing. I'm ready to go.'

'Then don't let me stand in your way.' He took a couple of steps backward and Lucy marvelled at his confident movements. Unless it was all bravado. He didn't want her to see him fumbling and stumbling. He had his pride. Too much of it. He was such a proud, arrogant man. He would do his suffering in private.

'I don't want to go,' she said, a sob in her throat. 'I want to stay here with you. I want to help you.'

He shook his head angrily. 'You don't know what you're saying. Haven't I just proved what a bastard I've turned into?'

'No.' She touched her hands to his chest. 'No, Conan. You're bitter and angry because of what's happened, but I understand all that. It's going to take a while to work things out, you have a lot of readjusting to do, but eventually you'll succeed.'

'But I won't be able to see,' he replied curtly. 'A minor detail, you might think, but have you any idea what it's like never to be able to see your face again, the expressions in your eyes, your mouth, those beautiful, kissable lips?'

'Your hands can be your eyes,' she murmured, lifting his hands to her face. 'Feel me, Conan, explore me...'

'Damn you, aren't you ever going to give up?' he demanded, jerking his hands furiously away.

'I love you, Conan,' she said determinedly, 'and I think you still love me. Please don't send me away. Your blindness truly makes no difference to how I feel. I——'

'But it makes a difference to how *I* feel,' he snapped. 'You seem to have difficulty accepting that fact.' His fingers were curled into fists now, and his jaw was tense, a muscle working spasmodically.

'Because I don't think you really know what's best for you,' she whispered painfully.

'I know,' he said, and it was just as though he was looking at her. It was an uncanny feeling. Lucy shivered. 'And getting you out of my life is my first priority.'

'I'm sorry,' she said almost soundlessly, and fresh tears coursed down her cheeks.

'Sorry for what? For me? Or yourself?'

'Both of us,' she choked. 'And I think you're making a big mistake. But if you won't let me stay permanently, then at least let me stay for a while. It's all new to you. Let me cook your lunch.'

His mouth tightened and he seemed to be fighting a monumental inner battle with himself, not liking to admit that there were things he could not yet do.

Finally he heaved a sigh. 'Until I can find myself a housekeeper, but not a moment longer. And keep out of my way, because I don't want your pity.'

'You haven't got it,' snapped Lucy, relief sharpening her voice, and then on a quieter note, 'I'm sorry if I was such a shock.'

'You thought I couldn't manage without you?' he sneered, his lip curling contemptuously.

'Oh, no, I don't think that at all,' she answered quickly. 'I think you'll manage just fine, given time. You won't let blindness get the better of you.'

'You're damn right I won't,' he snarled. 'I'll prove I don't need you. You nor anyone.'

Lucy remained silent. This could lead into a full-scale argument if she wasn't careful, and she didn't want to rile him any further. He would have no compunction about sending her away. She had got her reprieve, even if only for a few hours, and she must not spoil it.

'I'll go downstairs and make us a drink,' she said. 'What would you like, tea or coffee?'

'Scotch,' he said abruptly.

Lucy frowned. 'Is that wise?'

'I'll have what I damn well want,' he shot back at her. 'Are you going to get it, or shall I?'

'I will,' she said, deliberately keeping her tone calm. 'Are you coming down now? Can I——'

'I'm going to change,' he said. 'You go.'

Lucy hesitated. She was so afraid of him bumping into doors and furniture and hurting himself. He was in no mood to take things easy. But he would not want her to see him feeling his way inch by slow inch. Pride was a very powerful emotion.

'What are you waiting for?' he gritted. 'Me to make a fool of myself?'

'No, Conan. Of course not,' she said at once. 'I thought you might——'

'Need you? God, woman, haven't I made myself clear? I need no one.' His nostrils flared as his breathing deepened. 'Go and pour me that Scotch. I'll be down in a few minutes. And while you're at it, ring the domestic agency and ask them to send me a resident house-keeper straight away. Their number's in the book.'

It was more than a few minutes before Conan joined her. Lucy could hear him pacing up and down. At first she could not think what he was doing. She thought he must be trying to rid himself of his anger. Then she realised that he was probably familiarising himself with his room, counting his steps, making sure he knew exactly where everything was. It struck her how much was taken for granted when you could see.

When she heard him coming down the stairs she rushed out into the hall, anxious to lend him a hand should he need her.

'What the hell are you doing there?' he demanded, pausing half-way down and seeming to stare right at her.

'I thought, I wondered, I—er——' Lucy tailed off hopelessly. 'I'm sorry. It's just that I——'

'Find a blind man fascinating? Is it watching me feel my way, or is it my faltering footsteps? What is it, Lucy? Are you waiting for me to fall? Is that it? You want to prove yourself indispensable so that I won't send you away?'

Lucy's face creased in anguish and she gave a tiny cry of distress. 'Your drink's in the den,' she said, trying her hardest to keep her voice even. She retraced her steps back through into the cosy book-lined study. His father had told her that this was Conan's favourite room. She sat down in one of the easy chairs and waited.

Suddenly there was an almighty crash in the sitting-room, Conan roared, and Lucy shot to her feet. He lay sprawled on the floor. 'You moved a chair,' he accused savagely.

'I made a straight line through from the door to your den,' she admitted.

'And you think I would know that?' He was already pushing himself up. 'I had a picture in my mind of what this room was like. If you think that was helping me, Lucy, then you're badly mistaken. Please put the chairs back where they were.' He rubbed his shin, his face contorted with anger. 'I don't want you to move anything.'

Lucy obediently set the chairs back in their original positions, feeling hurt and foolish and almost like crying.

'Now, if you wouldn't mind pointing me in the right direction... Through your stupidity I've completely lost my bearings.'

She touched his arm and faced him towards the den. 'Now go and sit down.'

Lucy did so and refused to look at him as he made his way in. He would sense her pity, her eagerness to help should he put a foot wrong. Even in this short space of time he had developed extra senses that seemed to tell him even when she breathed.

'Where are you?' he asked.

'In the armchair near the window.'

Immediately he made his way towards the other chair, slowly, admittedly, but he seemed to have an excellent memory of where everything was, his hands seeking and finding, guiding him surely to his seat.

He sat down heavily. 'Now, where's that whisky?'

'On the low table to your right.'

He reached out and found it and drank the amber liquid in one swallow, pausing to savour the effect, and then saying strongly, 'I needed that. Where's the bottle? I could do with another.'

Lucy fetched the bottle from the cupboard and began to unscrew the top. 'I'll do it,' he said sharply.

She handed it to him and he carefully poured himself another glass, filling it slightly too full and spilling some on to his trousers. His face tightened. Lucy said nothing. He sipped some of the whisky, then fastened the top back on the bottle. 'You can put it away,' he said. 'I shan't want any more.'

All was silent for several minutes. Lucy was afraid to speak in case he snapped at her. It was so easy to say and do the wrong thing. She watched as he twisted his glass round and round. She wished he would relax. They were acting like strangers instead of being at ease in each other's company, happy he was out of hospital, planning their future.

Sadly, there could be no future, not unless he changed his mind. And how could she get him to do that? Another few hours and he would boot her out. They would never get together again. He would make sure of that.

'What are you thinking?' he demanded abruptly.

'Nothing.'

'That's impossible.'

'OK,' she shrugged, 'I was thinking about you, about us, about our future.'

He stilled and his fingers gripped the glass hard, and Lucy was afraid he would throw it at her. 'I'm sorry, but you did ask.'

'I think you'd better go and start preparing lunch,' he said.

'I think you're avoiding the issue,' she returned bravely.

'I've said all I intend saying on that subject,' he crisped. 'You know how I feel. I shall not change.'

Lucy swallowed hard and left the room. How difficult he was making it for her. Her eyes smarted with unshed tears. She wanted to get hold of him and shake him, and tell him what a mess he was making of his life. But she couldn't do that. He had to work things out in his own way.

All she could do was hope that one day he would realise that love did not go away because you were blind. He would realise that he still loved and wanted her, and she would be ready for him. It was all a matter of time.

She pondered on what to prepare for lunch. Something easy for him to eat? Or had he already mastered that art while in hospital? He wouldn't thank her for cutting his food into manageable pieces, that much she knew.

He was still very much a dominant male. He always would be. He was still virile and sensual. He still affected her like no other man ever had. Her skin warmed as she thought of his possession of her, and she could feel the adrenalin flowing. Suddenly she wanted him again.

It was a futile emotion unless things changed drastically between them. If she dared even kiss him he would reject her. And that hurt unbearably. She compressed her lips and began cooking their lunch.

The weather was still beautifully warm, so Lucy spread a cloth on the wooden table on the lawn, placing a bowl of roses in the centre, and when everything was ready she went to fetch Conan.

His empty glass rested on the table beside him, his eyes were closed, his legs stretched out, and he actually looked relaxed. The harsh lines in his face had softened, and she thought he might be asleep.

She touched his arm gently. 'Conan, lunch is ready,' and was startled when his hand shot forward and grasped her wrist.

'Kiss me,' he demanded.

Joy flooded into Lucy's heart and she willingly covered his mouth with hers. He had come to his senses. He was not going to send her away.

His hand came up behind her head and there was fever in his kiss, then just as suddenly he let her go and pushed her from him. 'I'm a fool,' he muttered thickly.

'For giving in to what is right and natural?' Her tone was soft and loving. 'No, Conan, I don't think so.'

'It won't work,' he thundered. 'I have to believe that.' He rested his head in his hands, his shoulders bowed, and Lucy wanted to touch him but did not dare.

Then abruptly he stood up. 'Let's eat.' A mask had been pulled over his face. It was hard and angular and controlled, and his moment of weakness had passed.

'I've laid a table outside,' she said.

She heard his swift intake of breath. 'Why is that?' he demanded furiously. 'So that I won't make a mess in the house? I'm not completely incapable, you know.'

Lucy flinched, but refused to let him know how much his harsh words hurt. 'I never thought you were,' she said levelly. 'It's just that as it's such a lovely day it seems a pity to sit indoors.'

Again that flare of nostrils, a sudden lifting of his chin. 'Lead the way.'

It was an uncomfortable meal, although it shouldn't have been. The weather was warm and sunny and still, the birds sang joyously in the trees, bees droned busily, and the scent of the roses filled the air. Everything was perfect, everything—except Conan's black mood.

'It's mushroom omelette,' Lucy said, setting his plate down on the table. 'And there are croquette potatoes on the left of it and green salad on the right. The condiments are in front of you.'

'Thank you.'

And they were the only words he said to her. Lucy toyed with her own food, not really wanting it, forking it around her plate, trying her hardest not to watch Conan. He was doing much better than she expected, even though some of the lettuce did slide over the edge of his plate.

It wasn't simply the fact that he said nothing that made the meal uncomfortable, but his attitude. He was ignoring her completely, rejecting her, shutting her out, and all because he thought it was the best thing to do. Not because he really wanted to. He had proved that by asking her to kiss him. Deep down inside he still loved her. But he would not admit it. He was bitterly proud. He saw himself as less than a man now, and under those circumstances he would not ask her to share his life.

'Would you like some ice-cream?' she asked when he had finished.

Conan shook his head.

'A cup of coffee?'

'Please.'

She went indoors and fetched the percolator, pouring their drinks, adding milk but no sugar to his, and then sliding the cup across the table towards him.

'Thank you,' he said, touching the saucer with his fingertips to acquaint himself with its position, before sitting back in his chair and turning his face up to the sun.

Lucy watched him, memorising every detail, the chiselled outline of his jaw, the beautiful shape of his brows, those thick, long lashes, his full, sensual lips. Just looking at them made her want to kiss him. 'Can't they operate on your eyes?' She spoke her thoughts without thinking.

'They could,' he admitted surprisingly, 'but I'm not willing to go through with it.'

Lucy stopped breathing. 'Why not?'

'Is it worth it if it's not certain it will be a success? Isn't it better to go on like this?'

'But surely they wouldn't operate if there wasn't a reasonable chance of you regaining your sight?' she frowned.

'It's not that simple,' he informed her drily. 'There were a lot of problems with shattered glass. Who knows what damage has been done? It might be best to leave well alone.'

'Your opinion, not the doctors'?' she asked scathingly.

'It's my head they're messing around with. I'm not sure I want them to touch it again. I almost ended up brain-damaged, Lucy. Do you know what that would have meant?'

She nodded painfully.

'Would you have still loved me?' he asked contemptuously.

'I'd love you whatever happened to you, Conan,' she said with feeling, her eyes luminous with unshed tears. 'When are you going to accept that?'

'Lucy.' He suddenly leaned forward towards her. 'I don't want you to feel like this about me. It's not going to work. I want you to put me out of your mind.'

'I can't,' she groaned.

'You must.' He stretched his hands across the table and she took them, and he squeezed her fingers so hard that he hurt. 'I'm no good to you now. I can't let you spend your life doing things for me. You deserve better.'

'I wouldn't be doing things for you,' she said. 'You've already told me that you're going to prove you don't need me. But I'm stubborn too, as you well know, and I'm not going to let you push me out of your life.'

Abruptly he let go of her fingers, and before she had realised his intention, before she could stop him, he swung his arm across the table and sent everything crashing to the floor. 'Damn you, Lucy. *Damn you!*'

'Was that supposed to be clever?' she demanded. 'What the hell do you think you're playing at?'

His breathing was ragged. 'Let's say if it wasn't those cups on the floor it would be you. You're trying my patience, Lucy.'

'By admitting I love you?' she asked huskily.

'Have you no pride?' he muttered thickly. 'Doesn't it mean anything when I say I don't want you?'

'Love has no pride,' she answered simply.

'So what do I have to say to make you go?'

'That you don't love me, but I wouldn't believe you. You're mixed up at the moment, that's all.'

'Maybe I am,' he shrugged. 'What would you say to a trial separation? Give me time to come to terms with myself?'

She eyed him warily. He had suddenly become too compliant. 'I don't think so. Once I'd gone away you'd probably disappear and I'd never find you again. And I can't live without you, Conan. I need you, even if you don't need me.'

'You need a man,' he scorned. 'A few months away from me and you'll soon find someone else.'

'No, I wouldn't,' she protested.

'I'm going up to my room to lie down,' he said. 'Let me know when the housekeeper turns up so that I can kiss you goodbye.'

There was heavy sarcasm in his voice, and Lucy clenched her fists. Had he any idea at all how much he was hurting her?

After he had gone she fetched a dustpan and brush and swept up the mess. The stainless steel percolator was dented badly and she doubted whether it would work again, the cups and saucers smashed beyond recognition. She tipped it all into the dustbin and then sat down again, her elbows resting on the table, her chin in her hands. What a day it was turning out to be.

The phone rang; it was the agency, apologising profusely, but they could send no one for over a week.

Lucy smiled as she began to plan what she would cook for dinner. She felt much happier, and even began singing as she peeled the potatoes. He had no excuse now for sending her away.

'Who was that on the telephone?'

Lucy whirled at the sound of Conan's voice. She had not heard him come down the stairs. He stood framed in the doorway and it was difficult to believe that he was blind. His eyes were as beautiful as ever.

She knew there was no point in evading the issue. 'The agency.'

His head jerked.

Lucy moistened her lips. 'They can't send anyone for at least a week. They're very sorry but they're fully booked.'

He swore explosively. 'Then try somewhere else. They're not the only bloody agency.'

'No,' said Lucy at once. 'You have me.'

'Damn you, I'll do it myself.'

Lucy's hopes fell, but minutes later he slammed down the phone, only he missed the handset and the whole lot went crashing to the floor.

She wanted to rush out into the hall and pick it up, but instead she let him do it himself, and when he came back into the kitchen he was in an even darker rage.

'Did you get someone?' she enquired sweetly.

'You know damn well I didn't,' he exploded.

'So what are you going to do now?'

'Throttle you with my bare hands,' he muttered savagely.

And the way they were curled at his sides Lucy knew he might easily carry out his threat. 'You could ask Mirry,' she suggested; not that she wanted the girl here, but it might look better if she appeared to be helpful.

His lip curled in a sneer. 'That really would be like the blind leading the blind. Use some sense, Lucy.'

'A week's not long,' she whispered encouragingly.

'Too long,' he rasped.

'Who knows,' she went on brightly, 'you might even find you enjoy being alone with me.'

She moved slowly towards him, watching him carefully, seeing by the way he took a breath that he knew she was approaching.

'I like the way you braille my body,' she said. 'And I'm sure you'll find out much more about me than if you were using your eyes.' She paused a few inches away. 'For instance,' she went on daringly, 'I bet you wouldn't see that my pulses flicker like mad whenever you're close. Nor would you see the heat of my skin, but you could feel it, and its texture. And you can smell my perfume, and feel my heart. Right at this moment it's going like a mad thing. Here, see for yourself.' She took his hand and placed his palm over her breast.

Lucy could feel the blood pounding in her head, and God, how she wanted him. She prayed that he would want her too. That he would see how impossible it would be for both of them if he sent her away.

But after a few seconds he freed himself. 'That won't work, Lucy. I know what you're trying to do. But I've made up my mind. Stay if you must, but keep away from me. Don't tempt me with your voluptuous body or I might just take what you're offering. But there'll be no love involved, just lust and anger and nothing else. And you might not find it quite so exciting as you imagine.'

Lucy felt tears begin to slide down her cheeks and she dashed them furiously away. 'You're a swine.'

'That's not all I am,' he sneered. 'Perhaps I ought to be thankful for this accident. You're seeing me in my true colours. You condemned me once, Lucy; do me a favour and do it again. That was the real me, taking your father to court, enjoying my prestige, not caring who I hurt in my power-struggle. It was my misfortune that I fell in love with you. It made me soft.' His chin jutted firmly. 'But not any more. If it's done nothing else it's made me see sense. I wonder how many men have been brought to their knees by a mere slip of a girl, and then lived to regret it for ever afterwards? I imagine I've had a close shave.'

Lucy clapped her hands over her ears. '*Shut up.* I won't listen to you. You don't mean it.' Her voice broke. 'I *know* you don't mean it.'

'Spare me the sob stuff,' he jeered derisively. 'I'm a hard man, Lucy, made even harder by what's happened. Stay at your peril. I have a feeling you'll live to rue the day you made the decision.'

If he acted like this all of the time, then she most certainly would. But this wasn't the real Conan, was it? It couldn't be. He was crazed by the trauma of discovering that he was blind. It had distorted his view on life.

'Conan——?' she implored.

'Lucy,' he mocked. 'What's wrong? Don't you like what you're seeing?'

'No,' she admitted, her voice no more than a squeak.

'Good, that's what I want.' His lip curled in yet another sneer. 'How much more do I have to say before you'll leave?'

'Conan, don't,' pleaded Lucy. 'I'm not going, whatever you say. But you're hurting me too much for me to stay here on my own. I'm going to ring Alan. He and my mother will both come, gladly, once they know you're home.'

'And you think that with our parents in the house I'll behave differently towards you?' he demanded arrogantly.

Lucy swallowed hard. 'Won't you?' Her question was no more than a whisper.

'My feelings will never change, Lucy. *Never!*'

'Nor will mine,' she said. But, sadly, now she knew what she had to do.

He had made it impossible for her. As soon as their parents arrived she would go. Not back to Derby, but to London. It was easy to lose yourself there. She would get a job, throw herself into it, make new friends, and push Conan right out of her life and out of her mind.

# CHAPTER TEN

VALERIE and Alan arrived in time for lunch the following day. Lucy ran out to greet them as soon as she heard their car. The last twenty-four hours had not been easy. Conan's attitude was inflexible, and she began to wonder whether he had ever really loved her.

Lucy did not see how he could change so dramatically. The accident should have brought them closer together, not set them apart. If the positions had been reversed she would have clung to Conan, someone safe and familiar, someone who loved her.

She opened the passenger door the moment Alan brought his car to a halt. Her mother climbed out and hugged Lucy. 'I'm pleased Conan's home. What wonderful news. So soon, too.'

'It was a surprise,' admitted Lucy.

'How is he?' asked Alan.

Lucy shrugged. 'Physically, there doesn't seem to be much wrong with him.'

'And mentally?' frowned her mother.

'He's having problems, but you'll find out for yourselves. He's waiting for you, let's go in.'

Conan was standing in the kitchen, his back to them, staring sightlessly out of the window. Lucy knew he must have heard them, because his hearing was so much more sensitive these days. He seemed to have trained himself, even in this remarkably short space of time, to hear things that other people could not hear.

'Son?' Alan went up to him and put his hand on his shoulder.

Conan turned, and the arrogance Lucy was getting used to had for once left his face. He looked tired and gaunt, though, and her heart went out to him. 'Father,' he greeted, and it was an effort to smile.

'It's marvellous they've sent you home so soon.'

'What's so marvellous about it when I can't see?' growled Conan. 'But actually, I discharged myself. I saw no point in sitting around there day after day.'

Alan was visibly shocked, and he raised a questioning brow in Lucy's direction.

She lifted her shoulders and spread her hands expressively. It was news to her, too.

Valerie moved forward and put her arms around Conan. 'You're alive, that's all that matters. We were so worried. Lucy never left your bedside except to sleep. I can imagine how glad she must be that you're out at last.'

Conan glanced coldly at Lucy. 'She's not staying.'

Valerie frowned and looked sharply at her daughter. 'I don't understand. You're deserting Conan? Why?'

'Because I have to,' said Lucy firmly.

'I think you and I need to talk. Come on, Lucy.' Valerie led the way to the wooden chairs on the lawn at the back of the house. She sat down, then looked sternly at her daughter. 'Now tell me what's going on.'

'It's simple,' said Lucy. 'Conan doesn't want me here.'

Valerie's head jerked. 'I don't believe that.'

'It's true.'

It occurred to her how young her mother looked. Marriage to Alan obviously suited her. She was radiant. Her hair was cleverly cut and she wore a green shantung silk dress that echoed the colour of her eyes. She was elegant and beautiful, and Lucy was proud of her.

'I thought you asked us to come down because Alan would want to see Conan. Obviously there's more to it than that.'

'A hell of a lot more,' confessed Lucy, her mouth tight.

'You say it's Conan who wants you to go? Why? I thought he loved you.'

Lucy sighed, her fingers twisting nervously. 'He's changed.'

'Because of his blindness?'

'Yes.'

'He needs you now more than ever.'

'He doesn't think so.'

'Then you'll have to persuade him.'

'You think I haven't tried?' she demanded. 'He's so proud, Mom, and so bitter, and so angry all the time.'

Valerie put her hand over her daughter's. 'It will pass, you'll just have to bear with him. Continue to show him that you love him and that——'

'No!' Lucy shook her head vigorously. 'He won't let me help him. I've told you, he wants me to go.'

'Perhaps it might be best for a while?' suggested her mother thoughtfully. 'His blindness is only temporary, isn't it? Dr Teal told Alan they could operate and——'

'Conan won't let them. The odds aren't too good, anyway.'

Valerie looked shocked. 'I don't believe this. Surely it's better to try and fail than not to try at all?'

Lucy grimaced. 'Tell Conan that. He has some bee in his bonnet that's going to take a lot of shifting.'

'I'll ask Alan to talk to him,' said her mother determinedly. 'This sort of situation cannot be allowed to go on. He'll listen to his father.'

'I wouldn't count on it,' snorted Lucy. 'I've cooked a chicken pie for lunch. Are you hungry?'

Valerie raised her brows. 'Subject closed?'

Lucy nodded. 'It's a pointless discussion. I've made up my mind to go, and nothing you can say will change it. You will stay until Conan gets a housekeeper?'

'Of course,' smiled the older woman. 'Now, there's plenty of food in the freezer and you'll——'

'I'm not going home,' cut in Lucy, 'I'm going to London. I'm sharing a flat with one of the girls I met at college. I phoned her last night, it's all arranged. I'll get a job there, and——'

'Lucy,' broke in her mother worriedly, 'are you sure that's necessary? Your home is with us, we——'

'And you'll do nothing but talk about Conan. Oh, no, Mom, I know what will happen. I'm going away and I'm going to forget all about him.'

'Are you?' asked her mother knowingly.

'I shall try. I know it won't be easy, but I don't see that I have any alternative. It took me a long while to learn to love him, and it will take me even longer to get over him, but it has to be done.'

'We'll see, love,' said her mother, and Lucy knew she was humouring her.

The conversation during lunch carefully avoided Conan's blindness and Lucy's leaving. They talked about music and the weather and how beautiful this part of the country was, and Lucy watched Conan carefully forking his food and admired the way he was coping. He really had no need to be sour; he was doing so well.

Alan offered to take Conan for a walk, and Lucy was surprised when he agreed. She had expected him to snap at his father. Perhaps it was only with her that he was short-tempered?

And so the day slowly passed, and the next morning Lucy said her goodbyes. She had had no more time alone with Conan, in fact he seemed to be deliberately avoiding her, and when she told him she was going he held out his hand as though she were simply an acquaintance.

Contact between them was electric. Didn't he feel it, too? She looked at his set face and wanted to scream out at the unfairness of it all. Why had this happened to them when they were so happy, when they had their whole future to look forward to? *Why?*

Impulsively she leaned towards him and kissed his mouth. He had not expected this and he jerked savagely away. 'Goodbye, Lucy.' His tone was cold.

'Goodbye,' she whispered faintly, and with tears streaming down her cheeks she headed for the door.

Valerie and Alan followed her outside and her mother hugged her tightly. 'I'm sorry, love. I'm sure he'll come round.'

'He won't,' said Lucy firmly. 'Goodbye, Mom. Goodbye, Alan.' She climbed into the taxi and was whisked away, and she did not even look back at the house.

London was hot and stifling after the open countryside. Lucy hated it. But Helen's flat was comfortable, and she even managed to find a job straight away as secretary to the Art Director of an advertising agency. And Dane Holt kept her so mercifully busy that she did not have time to think.

Unlike his previous secretary, Lucy did not mind working overtime; in fact she welcomed it, for work was her salvation. And Dane Holt rewarded her by taking her out to dinner when they had finished.

He was a short, fat, somewhat ugly man, and yet for all that she grew fond of him. Perhaps it was because he posed no threat. He was not interested in sex. He lived for his work and talked about it at all times. He was almost forty and had never married, and Lucy could see why.

Helen teased her about him. 'You need to watch that man. I'm sure he's not wining and dining you for nothing.'

Lucy laughed. 'He does it because he's grateful, and because he doesn't like eating alone, and because he likes someone to talk to. Heavens, he's so tied up in his work that I don't think he even knows what I look like.'

'Don't be too sure,' warned her blonde friend. 'One day he'll shock you and ask you to marry him.'

Lucy's eyes widened. 'It would indeed be a shock. He doesn't see me in that light.'

'No?'

'No! I'm his secretary and I do my work well and he appreciates it. Full stop. Nothing more.'

Helen grinned. 'Don't say I haven't warned you. Men don't take their secretaries out to dinner for nothing. He either wants an affair or he wants to put a wedding ring on your finger.'

'And you know that I'm interested in neither,' said Lucy firmly.

Helen sighed and looked at her friend sadly. 'Don't you think it's about time you forgot Conan? It has been three months, for heaven's sake, and in all that time you haven't been out with another man except Dane. If Conan had had second thoughts he'd have contacted you by now.'

'I realise that,' admitted Lucy, 'but I'll never forget him. I love him too much.'

'You're going to remain a spinster all your life because some stupid man takes it into his head that he's no good for you?'

'Conan's not stupid,' flared Lucy at once. 'He might be proud, too proud, in fact, but he's no fool.'

'No, you're the fool,' muttered Helen, and then on a more cheerful note, she said, 'How would you like to come to a party tomorrow night?'

'No, thanks,' said Lucy.

'But this one's different. There'll only be a few people there.'

'But you have an odd man and you want me to make up the numbers? Good try, Helen, but the answer's still no.'

Helen shook her head. 'I despair of you, Lucy, I really do. You're wasting your life.'

Lucy shrugged. 'So what? It's my life. I think I'll go and have a bath.' This was one of the few nights she was not working, and she intended having a lovely long, lazy soak. Helen was going out as usual, and she would have the flat to herself. It would be bliss.

In the early days after her flight to London Lucy had hated being alone, and she had phoned her mother frequently, anxious for news of Conan but determinedly never mentioning him, waiting instead for Valerie to bring him into the conversation, which she usually did. Lucy had once asked whether he had changed his mind about letting them operate, but her mother had said it was a subject she did not wish to discuss, and Lucy guessed that it had been the cause of many arguments between them. Eventually she stopped asking about him.

But, thinking about Conan now as she lay in the tub of hot, scented water, Lucy felt tears begin to slide down her cheeks. Life was so unfair. 'Damn you, Conan

Templeton!' she said out aloud. *'Damn you!'* She would never get over him. She loved him and she always would.

Christmas approached and Lucy allowed her mother to persuade her to go home. It would be her first visit since coming to London. 'Will Conan be there?' she asked, breaking her self-imposed silence about him.

'No,' said her mother, sounding sad. 'We did ask him, naturally, but he refused. He never leaves the house. Alan's desperately worried about him.'

'Is he alone?' asked Lucy, greedy now for any news about Conan, no matter how small. 'Did he get a housekeeper?'

'Yes, a nice lady, a widow, quite attractive.'

A shaft of jealousy shot through Lucy. How attractive? How old? Did he ignore his housekeeper as he had her, or did he use her to feed his masculine needs? The thought hurt. God, how it hurt. Lucy swallowed hard, and there was a painful lump in her throat.

'I see,' she said in a tiny, hurt voice.

She could almost see her mother's frown. 'Lucy, what's wrong? Are you upset because Conan won't be here? I thought you'd got over him. You never mention him any more. I thought——'

'I am over him, Mom,' cut in Lucy at once.

There was a few seconds' silence at the other end of the phone, then her mother said, 'That's all right, then. We'll see you on Friday, Lucy love. Alan will meet you at the station. Twelve o'clock, did you say?'

After they had finished their conversation Lucy told herself she was glad Conan would not be there, and yet deep down in her heart she knew that she wanted to see him again.

On Christmas Eve it snowed, feather-light flakes settling over the Derbyshire countryside, transforming it into a winter wonderland, a Christmas-card scene. It should have been perfect. Instead Lucy felt saddened.

Her heart ached because Conan was not here. Alan reminded her so much of him it was almost unbearable. But more heartbreaking still was the fact that if Conan had been here he would have seen none of this. She would have had to describe it to him. The snow-covered slopes, the trees with their frosting of white. It was breathtakingly beautiful. She wondered whether it was snowing in Hertfordshire.

On Christmas morning Alan phoned Conan, and Lucy heard him mention that she was staying with them. Whatever Conan's reply, it was disturbingly brief. He had probably said something like, 'Really?' decided Lucy. Or perhaps, 'What are you telling me for?' It was an effort to control the tears that stung the backs of her eyes.

'I'm sorry you're not here, son,' Alan went on. 'You do realise that this is the first Christmas we haven't spent at least a few hours together? How about if I come and fetch you tomorrow? I could set out early and be there by ten.' His lips compressed as he listened to Conan's reply. 'Of course the choice is yours. I'm sorry you feel like that.' He held the receiver out to Lucy. 'Do you want a word with him?'

Yes, she did. *She did*. She wanted to hear that deep, gravelly, sexy voice. She wanted to hear him say her name. It always sounded different when he said it. She wanted to ask how he was and what he was doing, but Conan had denied her all access to him. She had tried her hardest, but he had shut her out of his life and she must stay there. If he wanted her, he must make the first move. She shook her head. 'No thanks.'

'Merry Christmas then, son,' said Alan finally. 'Valerie and I will be down some time in the New Year.' He held the phone away from his ear as Conan said something sharply. Lucy could hear the deep, angry tones of his voice. 'Very well,' replied Alan, with more than a touch of asperity, 'but you're making a big mistake. It's easier to slide down into hell than climb out of it. If you won't help yourself, no one can do it for you.' With that, he put down the phone.

He returned to his seat. 'I will never, in a hundred years, understand that son of mine.'

'It must be a big shock to your system, knowing you can never see again,' said Valerie, putting a gentle hand on his arm, her love for him shining in her eyes.

'But that's the whole point. Why is he refusing an operation?'

'That, my love, I cannot answer,' said Valerie sadly. 'I don't think Lucy knows either, do you, love?'

'He's afraid,' Lucy admitted wryly. 'I know it's hard to believe, but he's got this dreadful fear that an operation will do more harm than good. Dr Teal told him that he was a hair's breadth from becoming brain-damaged, and he's convinced he'll end up even worse than he is now.'

'I didn't know,' breathed Valerie, her eyes distressed.

'He didn't tell me either,' confessed Alan, and he too looked near to tears. 'Not that I've seen much of him. He's become a hermit; he refuses to see anyone, even me. I knew how close to death he'd been, but not that an operation would be risky.'

This was one Christmas they would all remember for a long time. Lucy had not realised that Conan had shut himself away so completely. In fact she had half hoped he would be here, after all. She had even bought him a small present.

Talking about him, hearing the muffled tones of Conan's voice as he spoke to his father, brought Lucy's love rushing back to the surface. She had tried so hard to forget him, had kept her love shackled and buried, but now it burst free from its bonds and filled every inch of her body.

She could not go on like this. 'I think I might go and see him,' she said softly.

Alan shook his head. 'I'm sorry, Lucy, he was most definite about not wanting to see you.'

She closed her eyes, but this time the tears would not go away. They slid down her cheeks, and Alan pushed a handkerchief into her hand, and Valerie said with determined cheerfulness, 'Who's in favour of a Buck's Fizz?'

But no matter how much they pretended, Conan's attitude had set a damper on the whole holiday. Lucy was glad when it was time for her to go back to London. Helen was still away, visiting her own family, so Lucy had the flat to herself.

Dane Holt continued to work her hard and he continued to buy her dinners in compensation. Usually he dropped her off at her door, but one night he asked whether he might come in for a cup of coffee. 'I know it's late,' he said, 'but I'd like to talk to you.'

'Haven't we been talking all night?' she asked in some amusement. Dane never shut up.

'That was business,' he said. 'This is personal.'

Lucy felt a moment's apprehension, then she smiled and said, 'Of course, come on up.' Their flat was on the second floor of a large Edwardian house, with nice spacious rooms but not much of an outlook.

He followed her up the stairs and his breathing had deepened noticeably by the time they reached the flat. He really ought to lose some weight, thought Lucy, though she would never dare say anything to him.

'Here we are,' she said, pushing open the door, frowning slightly because the light was on. Perhaps Helen was back sooner than expected? 'Sit down and make yourself comfortable while I put the kettle on.'

'Wait, Lucy,' he said, catching hold of her arm, 'sit with me. The coffee was just an excuse.'

For once this extraordinarily ugly man looked nervous. A pulse flickered in his temple and there was a sheen of perspiration on his upper lip. Lucy had only ever seen him brisk and businesslike, and she wondered what was coming. Helen's warning drummed in her ears. But it couldn't be that, could it?

She sat beside him on the pink Dralon settee and he ran the tip of his tongue over his lips before turning to her and taking her hand. His palms were clammy.

'Lucy, I realise that this might come as something of a surprise, and I don't want you to give me your answer now.' His blue eyes behind the gold-rimmed spectacles shone in earnest. 'But—I—I'd like you to—to do me the honour of marrying me.' He saw the instant shock in her eyes and went on quickly, 'I could give you anything and everything you'll ever want. I know I'm not much to look at, but I do love you. I've never loved anyone else. I've always lived for my work.'

'Oh, Dane.' Lucy did not know what to say. There was no way she could marry him, but how could she say as much without hurting his feelings? Why hadn't she heeded Helen's warning? She ought not to have gone out with him so often. She ought to have known that there was a reason behind his invitations.

'As I said, Lucy, don't give me your answer now. Think about it. There's no rush.' Then he frowned. 'There isn't anyone else, is there?'

'No,' she said simply, 'there's no one else.'

'Good.' He beamed happily and then leaned forward and kissed her. It was no more than a planting of his lips on hers. It was over in an instant. And it meant nothing. Not to Lucy. Not a thing.

Had it been Conan kissing her she would have been set instantly on fire. She looked at Dane ruefully and stood up. 'I think I'll make that coffee.' And while she was in the kitchen she would think what was best to say. She would have to be careful, she could not be too blunt. If he was hard in business, he was sensitive where she was concerned. She could see that now and wondered why she had never spotted any clues before. What an idiot she was.

But the kitchen door opened before she reached it. So Helen was back and she had been in there all along. How much had she heard? Was she laughing up her sleeve?

It was not the other girl who emerged from the kitchen, though, but a tall man with black hair and dark glasses and a grim, forbidding line for a mouth. 'Conan?' she gasped. How ill he looked. How gaunt and drawn.

'That was quite a scene. I'm glad I witnessed it. It stopped me from making a fool of myself.' His tone was as hard as she had ever heard it.

'How did you get here?' Lucy's heart raced painfully with the shock of seeing him.

'I hardly think that matters now. I'm not staying.' And, with a curt nod at the man on the settee, he headed for the door. And they weren't the hesitant steps of a blind man feeling his way in a strange place.

'Conan, no! Wait!' Lucy headed him off and stood with her back against the door, her arms outstretched. 'You can't go, we have to talk.'

Dane Holt got to his feet and looked worriedly from one to the other. 'Perhaps it's me who should be leaving?'

'If you wouldn't mind,' breathed Lucy gratefully.

'This man, he's important to you?' asked Dane with sudden insight.

Lucy swallowed and nodded. The most important man in the whole world. 'We were in love once, until—something happened.'

'I see. It explains a lot. And I think I have my answer. Goodnight, Lucy, I'll see you in the morning.' He looked like a man who had lost everything.

She smiled ruefully and whispered, 'I'm sorry,' and moved to one side so that he could go. Then she turned to face Conan again, who had stood without moving while the scene with her employer took place.

'Who is he?' he snarled. 'I don't think much of your choice. What's his attraction, money?'

'He's my boss,' whispered Lucy, 'and I had no idea he felt this way.'

'But you have been out with him before? You must have encouraged him? An offer of marriage doesn't come out of the blue.'

'He takes me to dinner most evenings,' she admitted, her tongue cleaving to the roof of her suddenly dry mouth.

Conan's lip curled in a sneer. 'And you didn't realise what he was after? Come on, you surely don't expect me to believe that?'

'It's true, Conan, but it's not important. Tell me about you. You can see! *Oh, God, you can see.*' Tears filled her eyes and spilled down her cheeks.

'That's right,' he said coolly. 'But there's no need to get emotional. If I'd known what I know now, I would never have come. I was under the mistaken impression that you still cared about me.'

'I do,' she cried. 'Conan, of course I do.'

'I just heard you tell your—employer—that there was no other man in your life. That didn't sound to me like the confession of a girl who's still in love.'

'I didn't think you'd ever want me back,' she cried, a whole world of sadness in her eyes as she looked at him. 'I had to push you out of my life. After all, it has been over three months.'

His mouth firmed. 'I wasn't sane.'

'And now?' She hardly dared ask. But he had come here today, so surely it meant something?

'Let's sit down,' he said.

He dropped tiredly into one of their armchairs and Lucy perched on the edge of the settee, never taking her eyes off his face.

'How long have you—have you been able to see?' she asked tentatively, mentally crossing her fingers that the subject was not too disturbing for him to talk about.

'Hell, I don't know. One day runs into another.'

'I didn't even know you'd decided to let them operate.'

He leaned his head back, and it was almost a full minute before he spoke. 'I had to take the risk.' His voice was thick with suppressed emotion.

'Why?' she husked.

'Because of you.'

'Oh, Conan.' Her own throat felt full now. 'My love for you has never faltered. You didn't have to do it for me. I want you any way you are.'

He looked at her then. 'Do you? So why were you contemplating marriage?'

'I was not contemplating it,' she defended heatedly.

'Then why didn't you tell him no straight away and put the old buzzard out of his misery?'

'I wanted to let him down gently,' she said. 'I do have to work for him, don't forget. It's a good job. I don't want to lose it.'

'I bet it's good,' he sneered. 'What other perks do you get besides dinner?'

Lucy clenched her fists. 'Look, Conan, Dane Holt doesn't mean a thing to me. I was as shocked as you when he asked me to marry him. Do you really think I could let him touch me?' A shudder rode down her spine.

'I like to think not,' he said.

'And you'd better think that, because it's true,' she returned fiercely. 'So no more about him. It's you I want to talk about. You said you risked the operation for me. Does that mean what I think it means?'

'It means, Lucy——' and the words seemed to be dragged reluctantly out of him, 'that I love you and I've never stopped loving you.'

She was not quite sure whether he was looking at her, so she leaned forward and took off his glasses, and there in his eyes was a deep-seated pain, anguish so raw that it hurt her, too. She took his hands and they both stood and he held her close.

Words were not necessary, words would have spoilt this moment of love and comfort. Lucy had dreamt of such a thing happening, but had never dared believe it might come true.

He stroked her hair, his caress both a torment and a delight, and Lucy felt the tension gradually ease out of him. 'My love,' he murmured over and over again. 'Oh, my love, how nearly I lost you.'

'Please.' She put her fingers to his lips. 'Please don't say that.'

He kissed her fingers, one at a time, slowly and thoroughly, then he curled her hand in his palm. 'I couldn't see how you could possibly love a blind man. I thought you pitied me.'

'No, Conan,' she whispered, her throat aching with her love for this man. 'If you thought that, then you didn't know me very well at all.'

'I was crazed with pain and misery. I wasn't thinking straight.' His fingers tightened around hers, hurting her, though she was not even aware of it. 'I would listen to no one, not even my father.'

'He was hurt.'

'I know. And your mother said you no longer mentioned my name. I think she thought you'd got over me.'

'You hurt me so much,' she said.

His face creased in a fresh surge of agony. 'Don't.'

'I had my pride, too.'

'You deserved better than what I handed out. I treated you so badly.'

Lucy shook her head. 'You weren't yourself.'

'Not for a long time. I lived in a black hell. I never thought I'd get out.'

'So what happened?'

'We have Jenny to thank.'

Lucy frowned.

'My latest housekeeper.'

'Oh, yes, I've heard about her. A beautiful widow. What did she do?' Lucy did not realise that her tone had altered, or that she had stiffened in Conan's arms.

His lips twisted wryly. 'She brought me to my senses.'

'How?'

'By bullying me. God, did we have words! The times I've tried to throw her out and she wouldn't go.'

'Perhaps I shouldn't have gone?' queried Lucy softly, still feeling jealous of this unknown woman.

'Hell, no, if you'd stayed I would have destroyed you. There were no emotions involved where Jenny was concerned. She used to be a nurse in a psychiatric hospital. And boy, did she know how to treat me.'

Lucy said, 'I think I'd like to meet her.'

'Too late, she's gone.'

'So who's looking after you?'

He smiled, a real smile this time, one that reached his eyes and softened the gauntness of his face. 'The job's open.'

Lucy smiled too. 'Are you offering it to me?'

He nodded, looking very humble for so proud a man.

She turned her face up to his. 'In which case, I accept.' Tears of happiness shimmered on her lashes.

His mouth closed on hers in a kiss so tender that it aroused her more than any show of passion, and his hands moved gently over her, touching her ears and her hair and the flickering pulse at the base of her throat. His eyes looked into hers and they were filled with humility and love, and Lucy had never thought they would see her again.

'You'd had your operation when your father phoned you at Christmas?'

He nodded.

'Why didn't you tell him? It would have been the best Christmas present ever.'

'I was waiting to have my bandages taken off. I shouldn't even have been home, but I couldn't stand the thought of Christmas in hospital. Besides, I didn't want you to know. I'd planned this meeting for so long.'

Lucy suddenly frowned. 'How did you get in?'

'Your friend Helen sent me a key.'

'Helen?' she asked incredulously. This was a surprise a minute. 'She knew? How?'

'I phoned her.'

'So that's why she had this prolonged holiday? I wondered about it. Helen doesn't normally spend so much time at home. She doesn't get on with her parents.'

'She was very obliging. Said she'd be glad when I married you and took you off her hands.'

'Oh, she did, did she?' demanded Lucy in mock anger.

'She also told me you'd never had a date with another man. I think somehow she forgot to mention your boss?'

Lucy smiled to herself. She owed Helen a big thank-you. 'Dane doesn't count. I never saw him in any other light except as my boss.'

'Fortunately for you,' he growled. 'When you turned up here with him tonight I felt like knocking him flat. I was waiting for you just the other side of the door. I'd never been so excited or so afraid in all my life. What if I was wrong and you no longer loved me? There were so many unanswered questions. Then, when I heard a male voice——'

'You darted into the kitchen, leaving the light on,' she finished for him. 'I wondered about that. It wasn't dark when I went out, so I knew I hadn't left it on. I thought Helen must be home.'

'Lucy.' He looked serious again. 'I owe you another apology.'

She frowned at his grave expression. Now what?

'About your father. I acted too harshly. I shouldn't have taken him to court under the circumstances. But I didn't know about his heart condition, and at the time my firm needed the money we were owed in order to keep going ourselves. Can you ever forgive me?'

Lucy nodded. 'I've done all my hating. It's over now, and I've learned that bitterness never pays. Let's put the past behind us.'

He kissed her again, and Lucy's heart filled with happiness. 'I must phone my mother,' she said when he finally let her go.

He smiled. 'And I must speak to my father. I owe him an apology, too. I was pretty short with him at Christmas.'

'You ruined everybody's Christmas,' she reproved mildly. 'But knowing your sight's restored is the best present any of us could ever wish for. Which reminds me, I have something for you.'

He frowned.

'A Christmas present,' she grinned. 'I bought it just in case you turned up.'

'Oh, God, don't,' he groaned. 'Don't remind me what a selfish swine I've been.'

'Wait there,' she said, and dashed into her bedroom. She came out with her hands behind her back. 'Close your eyes and hold out your hands.'

Conan's lips quirked as he obeyed. It was small and quite heavy, and when he looked it was a tiny bronze statue of Zeus. He was seated on a throne with thunderbolts in one hand, ready to be hurled at his enemies, and a sceptre of cypresses in the other, and wearing a wreath of myrtle.

'King of the Gods,' she informed. 'Short-tempered and quarrelsome. He reminds me of you.'

'No more, my love,' he groaned. 'No more. I love you too much to ever risk losing you again. I shall put this where I can see it every day, and if ever I feel like hurling

PRISONER OF THE MIND

thunderbolts at you, I shall touch it, and remember, and kiss you instead.'

She grinned.

'I have something for you, too.'

Lucy's brows rose in surprise.

He put his hand into his pocket and pulled out a piece of paper. Lucy took it and looked at it and smiled radiantly. 'We're getting married tomorrow?'

'I'm afraid to wait any longer.'

'What if I say no?'

'You won't,' he replied confidently. 'I know you love me. Your doubts were in the beginning. Mine were in the end. I think we can both now safely say that we have a lasting love, a love that nothing or no one can put asunder.'

Lucy nodded, her happiness overflowing. 'I can't imagine life without you.'

'My love, my precious Lucy, you won't have to. Today we have found each other, and all our tomorrows will be spent together.'

She closed her eyes and he held her close, and her love flowed into him, and his love flowed into her, and whatever the vicar said tomorrow would make no difference. They were united. They were one now. They had climbed every obstacle, and a lifetime's happiness lay ahead.

# THE POWER, THE PASSION, AND THE PAIN.

**EMPIRE** – *Elaine Bissell* _____ £2.95
Sweeping from the 1920s to modern day, this is the unforgettable saga of Nan Mead. By building an empire of wealth and power she had triumphed in a man's world – yet to win the man she loves, she would sacrifice it all.

**FOR RICHER OR POORER** – *Ruth Alana Smith* _____ £2.50
Another compelling, witty novel by the best-selling author of 'After Midnight'. Dazzling socialite, Britt Hutton is drawn to wealthy oil tycoon, Clay Cole. Appearances, though, are not what they seem.

**SOUTHERN NIGHTS** – *Barbara Kaye* _____ £2.25
A tender romance of the Deep South, spanning the wider horizons of New York City. Shannon Parelli tragically loses her husband but when she finds a new lover, the path of true love does not run smooth.

These three new titles will be out in bookshops from December 1988.

## W⦿RLDWIDE

Available from Boots, Martins, John Menzies, WH Smith, Woolworths and other paperback stockists.